Unwritten King

Becky Titch

Contents

1. Diary of a Starving Artist

Nicholas was not a naturally quiet person, but very few knew this, and he was not one of them.

"Say, Nick, have you always been so shy?" prodded Ava Dubois, editorial director at the Seattle branch of Will & Williamson Publications, betraying an interest in what he had to say that she only ever carried under a specific set of conditions.

Speak-EZ Bar and Lounge, five P.M., company of twelve. The bar bore none of the mystery or class its name implied, brimming with wrinkled white collars and the stale scent of dwindling deodorant and unfulfillment. Red pleather peeled from the seats, the dim lighting was more an effect of age than aesthetics, and the jukebox in the corner – entirely the wrong time period – only had one working song. Every ten or fifteen minutes, a new patron would rise with a quiet exerted groan to insert a coin, and "Sweet Georgia Brown" would whistle from the speakers.

There was a slight tilt to every table. The largest seated six, which gave rise to an inevitable divide on the third Friday of every month when Floor Seven gathered for happy hour. One table seated the employees with 401(k)s.

The other, those they invited for politeness's sake, the way the older kids on the playground had allowed Nicholas to play a minor role in their games when he was young and loud enough to ask.

At his right sat the other editorial assistants, Conrad and Jane, leaning so close they looked like they were kissing from the right angle. Sometimes they were, and very noisily. To his left was Ken the intern, who did not seem to realize it was unusual to bring your best friend to an office outing as an intern, and said best friend, Connor. Nicholas had a feeling Connor knew but came anyway, because he was clearly in love with Ken. Then there was Ava, the only person at the table above the age of twenty-five. Nicholas couldn't place why she sat with them instead of pulling up a chair at the 401(k) table, except that she seemed to enjoy nosing into the lives of people young enough to be her children and looking down her long, narrow nose at their decisions. Probably because she didn't have any children of her own.

"Yes," Nicholas said, concise. She raised her beer and watched him over the misty glass, waiting for more. When she lowered it, there was pink all around the rim and a splotch of color missing from her pursed lips. Her brow took on a determined crease. He capitalized on her attention. "Do you remember that draft you told me you'd look over a while back? Do you have any notes for–"

Her focus shifted to Ken the intern with impressive speed. She said, like she'd been speaking with them all along, "And have you heard about the man from sales who got fired for disorderly conduct? Mary told me he faked partial paralysis so he could 'trip and fall' and peep under women's skirts several times a day. Surely there are better ways!"

Nicholas sighed.

"Legend," whispered Ken. Connor stepped on his foot. Ava didn't pick up on the interaction. Nicholas tended to catch things others did not; it came with the territory of being quiet, which came with the territory of being ignored.

He had lost his voice in much the same way he had lost his ability to walk for a short, blurry stretch when he was seven, after spending so many weeks halfway unconscious that his legs forgot their job. In a similar vein, and around the same time, those twin folds of tissue in his larynx had grown feeble. A voice had little use with no one around to listen. With help, his legs had remembered. Reticence, though, was a learned response, one he learned so well he assumed he'd always had it.

He devoted his memories of the first seven years of his life to his parents – their faces, their hands, their voices and how they lilted with inflections and accents – in a stubborn refusal to forget them. He didn't mind forgetting everything else. The version of him that spoke loudly and at length was as much a stranger to himself as to the coworkers at the table.

Accepting his rejection, Nicholas tuned in to the pair at his right.

"I just wanna..." Jane slurred, pushing back the sleeve of Conrad's blazer to pinch the back of his wrist. "I wanna peel your skin away and live inside it."

She leaned so far forward her seat started to tip. Conrad caught her by the back of the chair, and if the splotchy red on her face was anything to go by, she liked that a lot. Or she was just drunk.

"Yeah?" said Conrad. His glasses fogged up. "Yeah, babe, wear me like a dress. That way we'll never be apart."

Nicholas turned back to Ava.

"I love women!" Ken was protesting with broad hands splayed over his chest. This, Nicholas could attest. Ken loved frequently and deeply. Just that morning, he had come back from his coffee run with two trays of drinks and hearts in his eyes, mooning over the barista who put a smiley next to his name. Nicholas had plucked his own cup from the tray and chosen to withhold that it also had a smile.

"We all know you love women," crowed Ava. "But do you like women?"

"I'm not gay!"

Something seemed to dawn on him. Shock, then terror.

"Good grief, I'm not saying you're gay."

"I like women, and I'm gay," said Connor.

Ava laughed, shrill and toothy. "I've heard the two of you go on. If there's one thing gay men and straight men have in common, it's that they hate women."

She plunged into a long-winded tirade about men and women and the way men viewed women. It was surprisingly insightful, but Ken wasn't listening.

He sat unusually still, mouth parted like a screencap of low-budget horror. Slowly, movement returned to his face. A furrowed eyebrow, a shake of his head – denial. Twisting rage that drained into a wide-eyed plea directed at no one in particular. Ken went through what had been, for Nicholas, years of self-discovery in a matter of minutes. Before he could move to the next stage, he flinched as if he'd been struck, turning to Connor with a fishlike expression.

"You're gay?" he asked hollowly.

"Oh, did– did you not know?"

Nicholas watched their lives change with mingled amusement and in-trigue, long-since acquainted with the feeling of sitting at the very edge of something big, an observer just outside of its periphery. Ava was still ranting, oblivious.

Ken skipped over depression entirely, diving headfirst into acceptance. "Wanna date me?"

"Dude. Yeah."

Nicholas drifted back, behind his eyes, away from the passion spilling over onto his seat from both sides. If he squinted, there was something beautiful here. A sudden, life-altering awareness, a cyclone of confusion and realization, all at once slowed down, broken into digestible pieces by the person who'd been there all along. Nicholas liked that. He could work with that.

Reserved as he was at face value, his mind was rarely quiet. It was something a starving artist would say, the kind he would talk shit on if he were loud and a hypocrite.

Color bloomed on the backs of his eyelids. He let them shutter just long enough to get a clear image: rich greens and deep gray-browns, choppy rays of sun jutting between ancient leaves; the frontier between kingdoms, where his protagonist looked into the eyes of a man he'd once hated and thought: He's right, I can do this. I don't have a choice.

Nicholas liked that a lot.

"Excuse me," he said, abruptly rising to his feet. "I'll have to get going, now. Have a good night."

One half-hearted hum from Ava was all the response he got.

Jammed between his desk and his bed, with a reheated serving of pinakbet tagalog filling the only clear desk space and a steaming bowl of rice perched dubiously on one arm of his chair, Nicholas pried open his laptop. It whirred and clicked for an entire minute. He feared this might be the night it gave out, but it crawled up from its grave, quivering to life and emanating heat.

An unnamed folder at the top right corner of his desktop held four years of nights like these. Nicholas had come home to this same manila icon since he was seventeen. It had changed more than him. Even after he'd written the final chapter, he couldn't stop tweaking, revising, sometimes altogether rewriting.

Like he was now. By the time the idea bulging from his skull had turned into words on a screen that he was happy with, there was a throbbing pain around his eyes even though the brightness of his display couldn't get any lower. His pinakbet was unfinished and cold. It hadn't been right, anyway. It was his fifth time, now, trying to make it the way his mom had. He regretted starting so late, when the taste was no longer fresh in his memory.

Nicholas squinted at the time. Nearly three in the morning. He wondered whether his coworkers had sobered up before driving home.

He'd meant to study tonight. From the clutter on his desk, he picked out a book on intermediate Portuguese. He was blinking back sleep a few lines in.

"Not tonight," he muttered, conceding. "Right. Okay."

He rubbed the ache above his eyes and tried not to feel irritated. But he couldn't cook Filipino food and he couldn't make time to learn Portuguese, and all he had left of his parents was a dwindling savings account and the features glaring at him from a black computer screen. His laptop had died.

Brown skin from dad, soft cheeks and hooded eyes from mom; a wide, flat nose from the both of them, and hair that fell somewhere between his coils and her pin-straight. Maybe this was just another thing he was destined to live on the outskirts of. Nicholas shut the laptop and noticed behind it the small, unframed photo on the windowsill of his foster family smiling around him. It was so bleached by the sun, his skin tone matched theirs. Real fucking poetic.

An unanswered text was the only notification on his phone. It wasn't too late to reply, only a day or two. He glanced at it again.

Hey Nicky, been a while since

we heard from you. We

miss you. Get in touch when

you can, and let us know if

you ever need anything.

It wasn't that Nicholas had anything against Uncle Sam, who wasn't really his uncle anymore, or his wife and children.

But there had always been, since the day Nicholas was transferred from his first foster home to live with his ex-uncle, an air of moral obligation that even a nine-year-old could sense. After all, out of the five people in his parents' car when a drunk driver turned it into a hunk of scrap metal, Nicholas and Samuel were the only ones who'd made it out alive.

Nicholas had lost his parents and his only aunt. Samuel had lost his wife and in-laws. They were no longer related. Yet two years post-incident, when Samuel had recovered enough to take on a new burden, he'd tracked Nicholas down and moved him from Washington to Montana. Survivor's guilt, maybe. If he noticed that Nicholas was different these days, quieter, he probably attributed it to maturity or trauma.

In time, Uncle Sam had remarried and fathered kids of his own. His family had never failed to take care of Nicholas. They had been and still were very kind. They weren't his, though.

He typed out a short, noncommittal response before bed.

The bus stop across from his childhood library was only three blocks south of Will & Williamson. It was this convenience, not nostalgia or recognition, that had reintroduced Nicholas to Citlalli Aguilera.

He had yet to come and go without seeing her. If she wasn't hunched on a stool behind the counter scanning books in trembling fingers, she was hobbling between the shelves with a hand bracing her lower back. No matter where she was, she had an unnerving way of noticing him first.

She turned away from the prehistoric desktop's zoomed-in registry as he entered, peering owlishly at him through one brown eye while the other drifted lazily, clouded with cataracts. Her grin when she saw him was toothy, revealing several missing molars. Why she still worked at her age was beyond him.

Whatever the reason, he was grateful.

"Three weeks overdue," she chided before he'd stepped fully past the sensors. Straight to the point, as always.

He piled three books onto the counter before her with his most charming smile. "Ah, but all will be forgiven, hm?"

"There is a late fee, compounded per day."

"Oh," Nicholas said solemnly, casting his eyes down to the stack. Slowly, he raised his gaze, pleading through his lashes. "Surely you can make an exception for the starving artist who held on with innocent hands, naively unaware of this fee. Some mercy for this pobrecito?"

She leveled him with a narrow stare. "Did you translate that on your way in?"

"Would you prefer Portuguese?" Elbows propped over the books, Nicholas clasped his hands. "Please, Cici, for your coitadinho–"

She pulled the books out from under him. His elbows would probably bruise, but it was worth it when she said, "This is the last time. Do you feel good about the three dollars you steal from a dying public institution?"

"I feel so ashamed," Nicholas said, head bowed woefully to hide his smile. That ploy only worked about every third time.

Cici was smiling, too, ochre skin pulling taut and terribly fond over high cheekbones. "How did you find my recommendation?"

She dipped her chin toward the faded cover topping the pile. Act of False Faith, a short history on the forceful conversion of the Maya to Catholicism at the hand of Spanish Fransciscan Diego de Landa. At its heart was his notorious auto-de-fe, the bonfire burning of Yucatec canvases deemed demonic, and what it destroyed.

"Severely vexing," said Nicholas.

It wasn't the only book of its sort Cici had slid his way. She had a deeply-vested interest in massacred history: its motivations, its outcomes. The first title she ever recommended to him, back when he was six and could barely read, let alone understand its significance, had spotlit the Aztec codices destroyed by Itzcoatl. Back then, her diatribes were the best thing about library visits even though he'd struggled with her accent, and he had responded passionately in kind without knowing what he was talking about. He loved to listen to her still, though he was self-effacing with his opinions nowadays.

"Come, come see," she said, rising with a sound like snapping twigs. "We have new stock. Take your pick: Communist regimes or the Holocaust?"

"I am...very uncomfortable with this question."

"Book burnings, cariño, we're talking about book burnings. Suppression of dissent, control of information. I have two new titles."

"You could have specified, I think."

It was very possible that the sole reason she continued working was to sneak her passion into inventory orders and nudge patrons toward her picks. Maybe she felt a sense of duty, not just to her Aztec blood but to the words destroyed during the Chinese Cultural Revolution and the Spanish Inquisition, the stories left behind by colonial Africa and indigenous assimilation.

"History cannot be undone," she said on their way back to the counter, clutching a volume on Nazi book burnings. She either didn't realize or didn't care that she repeated this often. "Only destroyed and rewritten."

When the book was checked out (with a promise of timely return), she added, as an afterthought, "Oh, I finally looked over that story of yours."

Nicholas had been turning to leave. He did a sharp ninety degrees to lean across the counter on his forearms, startling her back a few inches. "Did you really? That's great! That's– what did you think? Did you read it all? How did you feel about Elias, I'm worried I rushed their relationship–"

"Take pity on these old ears. I can only process one thing at a time," Cici groused, though something knowing flickered in her paper-thin smile, faintly endeared.

That was a blatant lie. He apologized nonetheless, embarrassed by his outburst. Someone in the library was glaring at him, he could feel it, and he apologized to them, too, in his head. "Just. What did you think?"

"I thought it was good," she said. Nicholas swelled. "And that you could do much better."

Like a balloon with an unseen hole bitten through its neck, he deflated before he'd gotten the chance to fill. "It feels incomplete?"

"I do hope publishing is not on your agenda."

Nicholas eased off the counter. His eyes averted to the wide chalkboard near the entrance covered in markings, denser with scribbles near the bottom where more kids could reach. He didn't say that he wanted to publish his first novel as soon as possible, but she must have seen it anyway.

"You have what, twenty-one years? No rushing."

Nicholas bit his tongue. What else am I supposed to do? How long should I wait to be at the center of something?

That was the only reason he'd done any of this. He'd gotten a degree in English even though he couldn't stand the sorts of people that studied English, he'd thrown short stories at every local journal that might look at them, he'd interned and then worked under Ava fucking Dubois, all to get his foot in the door. And he'd always had this idea that the only obstacle was him and his nonexistent charisma, but if it was his writing – well, then–

"Nicholas," said Cici. "Calm down. You are more than talented enough to fix it."

She procured from somewhere beneath the counter the binder he'd given her some months ago. The paper inside was covered in red ink and crooked highlights. "The story is wonderful. But the world you've created feels very distant."

"...It's a fantasy," said Nicholas.

"And as the reader, I should feel so immersed in that fantasy that when I close the book I have to shake myself awake," said Cici. "Your setting and its magic are so far away, I wondered if you were having trouble visualizing them yourself. The story doesn't even have a name."

Nicholas didn't trust himself to speak without coming off defensive – as if he couldn't visualize his own world! – so he said nothing at all.

"I got this feeling, the further I read, that you do not know your characters very well."

His fingers twitched. He had powerpoints upon powerpoints about his characters. He had spreadsheets.

"What motivated their actions? Adrian ran away from his coronation, yes, he was not ready to be king, okay, but where did that sense of incompetence come from? How did it win out over the obligation he clearly feels toward his people? And your villain, Rayan, I'm not sure I've ever read a character so flat– does he have a reason for starting a war, or is he just bored? You need to get closer, mijo."

Nicholas had expected Cici's brand of brutal honesty. He had hoped for it. That didn't make it go down any easier.

"Alright." Nodding shallowly, he stacked the new rental on top of the binder. He was about to pull both away when another, bigger book was placed atop the first.

It looked and smelled centuries old. Its leather cover was blank and lifting up at the corners, bound front-to-back with a thin strap that wrapped around it several times. The pages inside had yellowed with age. They didn't sit entirely flat, curving against one another. Nicholas unwound the binding and found that they were empty. He looked up, bemused.

"A new medium might inspire you," said Cici. "There's no limit to what you may find when forced to translate your own words."

"You want me to put my story here?"

"If that is how you choose to use it," she said cryptically.

Nicholas trailed his fingers between two pages. They were surprisingly sturdy. He did it again, just to feel their texture. Rewriting one hundred ten thousand words by hand sounded like his personal hell on earth, but...he didn't want to let go of this journal, either.

"I wouldn't know where to start," he admitted.

Her smile took on the mischief of someone much younger. "How about 'Once upon a time?'"

Nicholas scrunched up his nose. "It isn't a fairytale."

"I don't see why not." She offered him a pencil. He took it, if only because his fingers itched to mark the page. They tingled, restless. He wrote in his best cursive.

There were no revelations, no light bulbs flickering on. But he loved how the pencil felt against the grainy paper.

"Are you going to say I should finish with 'The End,' too?"

"You've come this far, you might as well."

Nicholas kept toying with the pages, feeling the small gaps between them. He tested the smoothness of the spine beneath the pad of his thumb. "Thank you," he murmured. The journal was beautiful. He had half a mind to push it back toward her, if he wasn't so selfishly drawn to it. "For the recommendation, and for the notes, and for the gift."

She waved a dismissive hand. Kind crow's feet folded deep into her skin. "Off with you, now."

Nicholas didn't touch the journal for days.

Well, that wasn't true. He touched it plenty, couldn't seem to help himself – he skimmed his hand along the binding in passing, propped his wrist on the cover in the hours he worked unpaid overtime. But he hadn't written in it again. He still didn't know how he could use it.

Five days a week, eight hours a day, he sat in his unfortunately-placed cubicle and tried to work beneath the palpable tension cast from either side by Conrad and Jane, who were back to masquerading as acquaintances now that they were sober. Behind him, Ken swiveled his chair around every hour to show off borderline-NSFW pictures of his weekend tryst with his new boyfriend. And from her office in the corner, Ava continued to be conveniently distracted whenever Nicholas brought up the short excerpt she had promised to review.

Then he returned home, and he had all of Citlalli's notes to look over and sixty-thousand words worth of cuts to suggest on an impossibly thick manuscript by the end of the week. The journal would have to wait.

It was half-past ten on Friday when he sent in his edits. Yawning, he reached blindly for his binder and instead wrapped his hand around an unfortu- nate series of events: his forearm bumped his water bottle, an attempt to catch it somehow made it go down harder, and the precariously seated cap popped easily away. He hissed a curse and scrambled as water seeped through the pages, smearing the ink.

The damage wasn't extensive. Just a slow-growing patch at one edge that leached through the first several pages, ruining notes he had already gone through. There was no reason for his frustration to boil over, except that it had been bubbling at the brim for the last week and Nicholas was tired.

"Shit," he muttered as his nose started to sting. He didn't cry often, and certainly not over small inconveniences. If that was the case, he'd never stop. "Shit, God."

He scrubbed his sleeve under his nose and tried to push away from his desk, only to be reminded that there was hardly enough room between his desk and his bed for a chair in the first place. For a second, he was stuck, before he ripped himself out of the space and stumbled to his feet with another shout of, "Shit! It's fine, it's fine."

Relax.

Unwittingly, he reached for the journal. The cool leather was soothing to the touch; he grounded himself in its crinkled pages. Relax.

He settled on his bed before he could think too hard about it, turned on the yellow lamp on the stack of organizers he called his bedside, and began to draw.

It had been a while. His sketchbooks, gifts from Samuel's wife, sat untouched among the mess of his desk. He didn't have time for them, not if he was going to keep up with his job and publish before he turned twenty-four.

He could allow himself one break, though. Something about the vibrations when his pencil dragged along the paper soothed him like a balm, like the Vicks VapoRub his dad used to massage over his chest when he was sick.

He didn't pay much mind to what he was drawing or how much time he allowed to trickle by. An ethereal woman took shape, wreathed in darkness and blurry with anguish, reaching for a small, broken body at the bank of a steaming pond. The Lovers, he scrawled in the corner, right before his pencil slipped from his grasp and he succumbed to sleep.

He told himself it would only be that night, but he rolled over Saturday morning and buried himself in the journal. A new page came together like a connect-the-dots game, two figures floating side-by-side in a smudgy night sky like constellations. The same woman, this time made of stars, drifted with her lover. It didn't mean anything, but Nicholas liked it.

His next drawing took up two sheets and came from four years of imagining. A sweeping stone building cradled in a valley, abandoned and overgrown yet still so grand it could have been a castle. He labeled it Halcifer School of Magic, then scribbled a history into the empty spaces. He lifted his head late into the night with an aching neck.

On Sunday, he sketched rolling hills dotted by small, mossy homes. Primordial trees blanketed the landscape, thick with vines and flowers and life. A grazing beast here, a magical garden there, all leading toward a palace on a hill nestled between a massive rock arch and a waterfall that cast mist across its entrance. He titled this place Interra, straight from the pages of his novel.

He couldn't stop. He got home from work and made instant pancit canton and hovered over the journal with his fork hanging from his mouth. Over three nights, he reimagined Caldora, kingdom of mages. Four more, and he had sketched out every major character, crowded by bullet-list personalities and backstories. He moved on to minor characters, then invented beasts, then imaginary settings, and when he ran out of those, he started on the story.

It came to life like the old manga overfilling his shelves. Panels of action gathered on the pages with bubbles of dialogue and snippets of narration, presenting the most important plot points in chronological order. He drew fight scenes and first kisses, speeches and magic spells. How's this for visualizing? he mused.

When he showed Cici, all she did was laugh and whisper-yell, "Marvelous!"

Days bled into weeks bled into months. In the spare hours around work, Nicholas returned always to his journal.

It was another Floor Seven Friday when he practically burst through his apartment door, restless after the mere hour he'd lasted out with his coworkers. He kicked off his shoes and squeezed onto his chair with his work bag still slung over his shoulder. He hadn't had a sip to drink, but he was tipsy with excitement.

He turned past his most recent page, pausing to admire the image of his villain hanging several feet from the floor in a listless arch, gouged through the chest by a thick, spearlike stalk.

His next drawing would be the last.

He'd been distracted all day at work, debating which scene of the resolution he wanted to realize. He landed on this: Adrian, his hero, wrapped in his lover's arms on a palace balcony, stories above a joyous celebration, his rightful crown draped over his forehead.

For the sake of the joke, he wrote beneath it, The End. He looked proudly down at his work. He had really finished.

I really finished.

His smile slipped in increments as he studied those final words.

It occurred to him, with his pencil still lingering over the period, that he didn't feel any closer to the smiling faces on the page than he had the day he received the journal.

He didn't get time to dwell on it.

The moment he let the pencil fall, an invisible force yanked Nicholas' hands flat over the open pages. He was allowed a quarter-second of alarm, of rounding eyes and a cut-off gasp, before a feeling like pressing your palm to the mouth of a vacuum hose sucked him to the desk. Nicholas tried to scream and found his mouth submerged in– submerged in the book. He was choking, yellow-beige obscuring his vision as his face rapidly sank and his body curled forward, squeezing. Somewhere in the midst of warring confusion and panic, he reached a shocking point of clarity – either he was dreaming, or he was going to die. He would wake up slumped over his desk, drooling on the pages, or he would be crushed beneath this impossible pressure and disappear inside them.

Everything stopped, and for an instant he was suspended in nothing.

Then he hurtled forward. Or maybe he was stuck in place, and everything was hurtling past him. Pencil scratches curved around every inch of his view at breakneck speed– a lover's death at the shore of a pond– darlings written in the stars– a castle of a school– a lush landscape, the first burst of color, green. He felt the brush of a leaf against his cheek and tried again to shout, voiceless. Images rushed by too fast to process, each more material than the last. Suddenly there was fire– no, pain, scorching his abdomen, forcing his eyes shut and dragging a haggard scream from the depths of his chest. It hurt so badly, he didn't even notice that the sound made it out of his throat, or that the hurtling had stopped, or that his knees and palms were scraping harsh stone.

Nicholas coughed and tasted iron. There were startled voices somewhere past the ringing in his ears, maybe far away, maybe right on top of him. He blinked and got a bleary glimpse of a city that was most certainly not Seattle. Under any other circumstance, it might have been familiar. As it was, that short glimpse was all he got before the pain reached a crest and his vision went black.

Rough stone. Chilly air against hot skin – not burning, but fevered. The smell of earth and rain and something stale, a mustiness that tickled his nose. Nicholas slowly blinked away the crust sticking his eyes together and saw dark steel wheels– no, disks– no, eyes, glaring down at him. Gray eyes, cold as metal. He knew those eyes, how did he know them?

"Not yet." The mouth beneath the eyes was moving; the voice that came out was just as crisp. Everything about the face was impossibly familiar. Cool fingers pushed Nicholas' eyes shut, something touched his nose, and he slept.

2. Too Close For Comfort

The next time he opened his eyes, Nicholas was looking at a girl.

She appeared in bits and pieces as his vision came into focus: olive skin over a strict face framed by straight sheets of wine-red hair, nearly black eyes narrowed at him. His view shifted as something turned his head side to side.

"Yasmin," Nicholas murmured. He sagged with relief; he was dreaming.

He'd never felt pain in a dream, though.

"How do you know my name?" demanded the girl. Yasmin. His Yasmin. Her voice was deeper than he'd imagined and carried a slight accent he hadn't anticipated, gently semitic. The rest of the scene came to him slowly. Nicholas was in a small wooden room dimly lit by mounted candles. There were no windows and one door. He was sitting in a chair while Yasmin stood between him and a table, leaning down to his eye level.

He was hurting in a lot of places. His entire torso felt tender and hot, like he had been burned from his hips to his chest. There was a stabbing pang in his right ankle. He tried to wiggle it and gasped out, folding forward to cradle it. His shoulder jerked uncomfortably - his wrists were bound behind the chair.

"I asked you a question," said Yasmin. There were pinpricks of pain on his chin, too, where her nails dug into his skin. "Who are you, why are you here, and how do you know who I am?"

Nicholas hadn't known a lucid dream could be so vivid. He squeezed his eyes tight and willed himself to wake up before it became a nightmare.

He felt a frustrated huff of air against his cheek. The touch on his chin disappeared, and his head drooped for just a second before whipping to the side with a sound like a cracking whip. Nicholas' eyes flew open as he sucked a haggard breath, spitting blood where he'd bitten his tongue. Heaving, he lifted his head. His cheek burned. He could feel four gashes in his skin like claw marks. Yasmin made a show of turning her four rings around so the fat jewels and filigree were facing the inside. A droplet of blood trickled down her palm, the same color as the polish on her long, pointed nails.

"So you can open your mouth," she sneered. "Tight lips will cost you."

"I- I don't..." Nicholas gaped up at her. He felt like his skull was still rattling. "I don't know what's happening."

Bearing down on him was a woman who did not exist. Yasmin, former military captain turned no-nonsense bodyguard to the king. The king of Caldora. Every line of her, from the hair to the nails to the military badges on her tailcoat, had lived for years in his head, then in the journal. She was a fictional character from a fictional land. There was no feasible way she could stand before him in the flesh. But that slap had felt very, very real, and if the shock of it hadn't woken him up, then-

Then he wasn't dreaming.

"You've been arrested under suspicion of espionage," Yasmin said simply. "Your turn. Or are you going to make me ask again?"

His next breath came shallower than the last. "My name is Nicholas," he hurried. "Nicholas Lao Batista. I don't know how I got here, I don't know how it's possible, I-"

Yasmin grabbed his chin again, yanking his head as far as his neck would allow. "Two options, Nicholas. You can make this easier for both of us- tell me who sent you and what you're meant to report. Or you can resist and force me to waste my time here with you. Take your pick. Quickly."

"I'm not trying to resist!" Nicholas managed around the rapid rise and fall of his chest. "Please, I'm not- I'm not supposed to be here- I'm not a spy."

What's happening? he thought, over and over, faster with every uptick of his racing pulse. What's happening, what's happening, what's happening?

With her thumb, Yasmin swiveled the ring on her little finger, twisting it all the way around. "I'll ask you one more time. Who sent you?"

"No one! No one, I swear-"

She slapped him so hard his neck cracked. The gemstones tore into his flesh, leaving a ravaged mess behind.

"Please." His blood rushed in his ears. "Whoever you're looking for, it's not me."

He was already gasping for breath when her fist slammed into his gut. Nicholas coughed, wetting his chin, sucking in air just to retch it back out.

"That's enough."

It was a new voice, and it came from behind him. Yasmin looked over Nicholas' shoulder, an irritated twitch to her lips, then straightened, dropping her head in a bow and edging away from the table. "As you wish."

If Nicholas wasn't seeing spots and on the verge of hyperventilating, he might have put the pieces together at the first click of a heeled boot behind him. He might have remembered that there was only one person Yasmin deferred to before the first pant leg came into view, hugging a slender, impossibly long limb. Nicholas looked up and saw a coat that swept down to the knees, glimmering with shining embroidery where the light hit it, pulled over silk gloves and a matching vest. All of it black, save for silver buttons and five gemstone rings.

It clicked just before Nicholas arrived at a pale face. Half of it was cut with shadows, turning sharp features severe, but Nicholas knew him.

Nicholas choked out a delirious laugh. Just his luck - King Rayan, the ruler of Caldora and the villain of his story.

"Is something funny?" asked the king, towering over him. He had it too, that unexpected accent.

"No," Nicholas rasped. "Sir."

Rayan didn't respond. He didn't say anything at all. The room would have been quiet if not for Nicholas' panting. With every passing minute, it evened, until he was breathing shallow but steady. The panic ebbed and flowed before slowly draining away, leaving behind wintry dread. Nicholas shuddered.

"Let me explain the situation to you, since you don't seem to understand."

You've got that right, thought Nicholas, mildly hysterical. Rayan crouched, and Nicholas saw close up the ashen circles under his eyes, the slight hook to his nose that Nicholas and his eraser had agonized over for hours.

"A stranger in unfamiliar garb appears out of nowhere carrying foreign objects and leaves a crater in my city square. Nothing on his person suggests Caldoran birth, and the only sign that he has ties to us at all is his diary." Rayan reached behind himself onto the table. Nicholas watched, horrified, as his journal came into view, held loftily in spidery fingers. "In which I meet my gruesome end. Thanks for that, by the way. I have to ask: if you're as innocent as you claim, how did you depict me so well?"

He opened his other hand face up as if to ask for something. A small flame appeared, floating above his palm, expanding and shrinking with every inhale and exhale. On the hand holding the book, the ring on his middle finger flickered with a faint spark, a power that came from deep within the crimson gem at its center.

Vigalis - energy ore. Nicholas was probably losing his mind, because his first thought was, I never thought of making it glow. That's a good idea.

His next thought was: fucking hell, he's going to burn me.

Rayan held his palm up and toyed with the flame, twirling it between his fingers. It dwindled to the size of a penny and rolled to the tip of his index finger. He pointed it at Nicholas, then flicked it back toward his palm and opened his hand. The flame grew as big as his head in an instant, just shy of licking Nicholas' nose.

Rayan shrank it down to the size of a ping pong ball and bounced it from finger to finger. "Ten. Nine. Eight..." he muttered with each exchange, like he was tallying his movements instead of counting down the seconds until his patience ran out.

Seven left. Nicholas used five of them to run through his options and their outcomes.

He could keep telling the truth and get a ball of fire to the face. Or he could tell a bigger truth, the whole truth: that he was a writer from another world who had somehow gotten transported into his own book. And then what? Rayan would call him a liar or call him insane. Or maybe, somehow, he'd believe it, and he'd have the man who wrote his death at his mercy.

"Four. Three."

The heat of the flame stung his cheek.

Nicholas' sixth second was wasted by crippling fear, the kind that slammed his whole body and filled his head with fog. He'd felt this once before, in the fraction of a second before the crash that killed his parents. It was the specific feeling of seeing immense pain coming and being helpless to stop it.

He braced for it in the seventh second, shutting his eyes tight. Fat, mortifying tears squeezed out. He opened his mouth to say something, anything, to buy himself some time.

The heat disappeared.

Nicholas canted forward with the force of the breath he'd been holding. Through misty eyes, he saw the king stand. The fire was gone.

"Ray- Your Majesty," said Yasmin.

"Quiet," commanded the king. Then, to Nicholas, "Twelve hours. Decide in that time where your priorities lie."

He swept two fingers. Every candle in the room went out except for the one by the exit. Yasmin made a lazy flicking motion with her hand and the door swung open. Two men in gray uniforms stood outside.

"Take him downstairs," said Rayan. He left with his bodyguard in tow. It would have been a very cool dramatic exit if not for what sounded like an angry whisper from Yasmin and an answering grumble from the king. Nicholas couldn't make out the words. Their bickering receded down the hall.

Downstairs, it turned out, was a jail.

He got a cell all to himself, in a corner next to a man whose tattooed skin hung off his bones like baggy clothing and across from a woman engrossed in heated discussion with an albino rat. They both turned their heads as Nicholas was ushered, limping, into his cell. The woman and the rat, that is.

"What did you do?" she asked, leering at him with big glassy eyes as he settled gingerly onto the cot in the corner. Mousy brown hair fell in strings down to her hips. Her age was impossible to guess.

"Nothing," he said miserably.

She gave a scraping laugh and tipped backward onto the floor. Her rat friend scurried onto her chest. Throwing her hands above her head, she cried, "Do you want to know what I did?"

Nicholas turned his back to her. Facing the wall, he took stock of himself and his surroundings.

"It was her! It was her, but I'm here, and isn't that fucked?"

The cell offered maybe forty square feet of space, most of it taken up by the cot and the ominous hole in the corner. The air was dim and wet and cold and carried a stale smell like damp earth, without any of the nostalgia of summer evenings spent hopping from puddle to puddle. Still, it was familiar somehow, like he'd been here before.

"She asked me for love!" the woman professed to the ceiling. "Love, love - what a pure thing to ask for, love!"

He was still in his work clothes, except for the shoes he had left in the front hall of his apartment. He was sure he'd had his work bag with him when he...well, he still didn't know what he'd done. But his bag was missing and his pockets were empty. He patted them down feverishly, like his wallet may somehow appear. It was gone, which meant the picture of his parents in the front sleeve was gone, too.

"So I gave it to her! Love in a bottle, how precious! I gave it to her and he drank it and she couldn't handle the way he loved her, and do you know what she did?"

Nicholas' lips were cracked and crusted in the corners with dried blood. The entire left side of his face was sore, warm around the gashes in his cheeks. Wincing, he stretched out his right leg. His ankle had swollen so badly he couldn't move his foot at all. It throbbed with a deep, measured ache. But what hurt the worst and scared him the most was the mysterious pain at his abdomen.

"You'll never believe it. Really, you won't! I still don't believe it! Are you listening?"

He untucked his shirt from his slacks and started on the buttons. After the fourth, he could make out blistered skin. Just narrow strips at first, then broader pink bands that clawed up from his hips. He hissed every time his shirt brushed against them. Heat radiated from the wound, enough to feel on his fingers even though he avoided touching it.

He didn't know where it had come from. That was the part that scared him.

"I hate men who don't listen! I hate them, I hate them, I hate them I hate them I hate you! Oh, but I love telling stories, and you love listening. I can sense that in you. Okay, okay, I'l tell you!"

Well, that and the fact that he was currently behind bars in a made-up world, held captive by a villain that he had described in his spreadsheet with words like cold and ruthless.

"She called me a witch!" the woman shrieked. "Not to my face, oh no, she could never be so bold. She called me a witch to the graymen and they-they- they took me! And you know the fate of a woman called a witch. You know, I know you know. God, say something. Don't you feel sorry for me?"

Nicholas finally glanced over his shoulder and found her holding the bars of her cell, pouting ghoulishly at his inattention. "I'm sorry," he said. Satisfied, she flopped back down.

Graymen. The Caldoran police, the same people who had dumped Nicholas in his cell. He had designed their uniforms painstakingly, down to the steel tips of their boots and the scrunch lines of the pants tucked into them. He knew them well.

A witch, though. That was new to him. In all of his spreadsheets and documents and drawings, he had never mentioned witchcraft. As far as he knew, the world he created didn't have things like love potions.

He'd never written anything about a jail, either. He looked down at the red marks on his wrists where the rope had pulled too tight and tried to process that there was much more to this world than what he'd put down. Considering he was still struggling to process that he was here to begin with, it went okay.

It helped that he didn't have a choice. Whether he'd been transported to another world or trapped in a vivid dream, either way, some sort of magic was at play. There was no use denying it.

So. Magic was real.

"Okay," he mumbled. "Okay."

"What?" shouted the woman.

Magic was real, and he was inside it. It was any fantasy lover's dream come true. His dreams had never looked quite like this, though. *You need to get closer, mijo,* Cici had said, but this felt a bit on the nose.

In all of this, that was the hardest to wrap his head around. Not that Cici owned a powerful ancient journal that could swallow people into their own stories; if anyone on Earth was going to have magic like that, it would be her. The part that was hard to swallow was that she would betray him like this.

He'd thought of her as his friend. His only friend. But she'd gone and given him that stupid fucking book knowing what it would get him into - and she must have known, he was sure of that much. No warning, no asking if it was what he wanted. She had tricked him with a leathery smile on her face, and for what? Why would she send him here? What if he died here? Could he die here? It sure felt like he could.

Would she even care?

He had no idea how big this world really was, or how to get out of this situation. He had no idea how to get home.

Nicholas tried to hug his legs close and hissed from the pain. Everything hurt. He settled for scooting carefully into the corner to lean his temple against the cool wall. That was where he stayed as the other inmates filed down the cell block for dinner. It was so quiet when they left, he could hear the drip, drip, drip of leaking water.

Twelve hours, the king had said.

Nicholas' best imaginings couldn't have conjured up Rayan's voice. He'd envisioned something molasses-smooth, and he hadn't been wrong, but it was coarse around the edges, too. A broken piece of ice, the sort of penetrating cold that you flinched away from after one touch but felt in your fingertips for minutes after. Nicholas was still shivering, and it had been…

How long had it been?

He had to somehow convince a merciless king to pity him, and he didn't even know how much time he had left.

Just come up with something, he urged himself. You're a writer, you can do this.

Nicholas could not do this.

His best bet was to deny all responsibility. This freak journal just wound up in my hands and brought me here. I'm as lost as you are! No, I don't know why my name is written inside the front cover. Seriously, I'm so so boring and standard. Substandard, even. I could never be a spy! I wouldn't kill you like that, really sir, you don't deserve it, there must be someone extremely evil and lame behind this. Now that we've cleared that up, could you please help me get home to another world?

Mediocre probability of overall success. Low probability of ensuring his safe return home. Zero probability of relinquishment of the journal, which in turn brought the chance of safe return to zero. If the journal had sucked him in, it had to be his way out, too. He needed a way to leave and take it with him. He needed a plan, and fast.

The thing was, Nicholas was the kind of writer who took two months just to outline a getaway scene. He didn't do fast plans. He didn't know how much time he had left, just that the only noises along the cell block were the snores of his neighbors and the albino rat's fevered scuttling.

Maybe he could charm the king into setting him free. Nicholas laughed out loud. The rat's glowing red eyes snapped to him and he shut up. He felt the urge to cry again. He was definitely losing his mind.

The rat scurried under the woman's bed at a distant popping sound. Somewhere Nicholas couldn't see, a door scraped open. After a beat of silence, there were footsteps; sharp, hurried, and quickly drawing near. Nicholas went rigid. It couldn't have been twelve hours yet. A silhouette appeared at the end of the block, casting a tall, feminine shadow nearly to his cell. Bile surged in his throat. He would've been sick if he'd eaten.

"Is," His voice failed him. It was probably drowning in all the bile. He tried again. "Is it time?"

On the other side of the bars, Yasmin looked like she wanted to smite him. Her left eye was twitching. "Not quite," she said through her teeth. "There's been a change of plans."

3. The King and His Men

Nicholas didn't normally mind silence, and rarely tried to fill it. But this - sitting handcuffed in a carriage with a woman who glared fire and brimstone whenever he so much as breathed too loudly - was excruciating.

He made the mistake early on of trying to ask where they were going. Yasmin snapped her head his way with hellfire in her eyes, and he decided to cut his losses after the first syllable. She sat as close to the door as she could without pressing her body against it, like Nicholas was diseased or smelled horrible (which, after the day he'd had, was probably true). It was the longest carriage ride of his life. Also the only carriage ride of his life.

The window to his left let in a midsummer breeze. He rested his head and let it kiss the wound on his cheek. It stung a little, but it was warm, and it was gentle. The city passed by slowly, and Nicholas watched it, eyes wide to take in everything he could. It was exactly like he'd imagined, long roads paved with stone and lined by tudor-style houses. He could only see what fell within the shifting circles of orange cast by the streetlights. Atop the posts were magical flames encased in large spherical bulbs. He had never considered, when he drew them, who lit the fires every night. Now he wanted to know badly.

There was a lot he hadn't considered. The Caldora he'd dreamed up was a bustling nation overflowing with magic and bad intentions, all of them aimed at its rival kingdom, Interra, home of his protaginist. But right now, at least, it was exceptionally quiet. Caldora in the dead of night was peaceful.

There was someone living in every one of those narrow homes. Maybe multiple someones. There were personalities and wants and kinships here he hadn't spared a second to dream up. There was life here, outside of his head, all around him. It was too much.

Something light fell onto Nicholas' lap. "When I tell you to, cover your eyes," said Yasmin.

He fumbled with bound hands to pull the knotted cloth over his eyes. The darkness was total, and he was relieved.

"Or do it now."

After a few minutes, the air started to change. It was cooler, a bit wetter. He slipped a finger beneath the blindfold to pull it away from one eye and lost his breath. Through the window at the front of the carriage, so huge and so near he couldn't see the tips of it, was the king's castle. In a way, it resembled its ruler: tall, angular, and grayscale. It was asymmetrical and foreboding. High towers with steep prism roofs scraped the clouds, pointed arches climbed from the ground - looking at it on a page, Nicholas had never noticed the way it seemed to claw for the sky.

The blindfold fell away to hang around his neck as he strained to glimpse Lake Charlatan. It surrounded the castle on three sides and seemed to go on forever. He hadn't known he could make something so beautiful.

"Eyes," Yasmin said as they approached the gates. He was reluctant, this time, to cover them.

The carriage rumbled to a stop on smoother ground. Nicholas could guess where they were; he mourned that he wouldn't get to see the castle from the inside. The door opened and he nearly tumbled out of the carriage. Sharp nails came down on his shoulder, forcing him forward, and he was abruptly reminded that he had bigger things to worry about.

He was led, hobbling on his injured foot, down chilly halls. Yasmin was pitiless. She moved briskly despite the pained huffs catching behind his teeth. He committed the path to memory as well as he could: right turn, right turn, left turn, straight for a while, stop. Nicholas was not one to waste his time on futile hopes, and escaping from a castle manned by powerful mages was the very embodiment of a pipe dream, but he wasn't normally faced with life or death, either.

By the time Yasmin pushed him through a doorway, his forehead was beaded with sweat. She kept going until his thighs collided with something soft. "Sit," she said, and he dropped immediately onto his forearms on what felt like a mattress and took the pressure off his foot. A match was struck, then two locks clicked; first, the door at his back, then the cuffs around his wrists. They dropped away, and Yasmin said, "You may look."

He tugged off the blindfold and beheld bare wooden walls. He could only see a small square of the room, the rest hidden behind a white curtain. The bed he slumped over was surprisingly plain and narrow for how plush it felt beneath his elbows. He hauled himself onto the colorless sheets, turning to sit facing Yasmin, and waited.

But Yasmin did not say anything else. Without looking away from Nicholas, without moving at all save for the waving of her fingers, she rummaged through the only other furniture in the room. The cabinet door swayed open and an assortment of items floated out onto the counter beneath it. Faint glacial blue gleamed from the ring on her pointer finger.

A labelless black bottle and something white drifted toward Nicholas. He scurried away on his hands, but there was only so far he could go. The cap of the bottle twisted away. Clear liquid dripped over a square of gauze. "Wait, what are you doing?" He leaned back as much as gravity would allow. Yasmin took no interest in his terror. "Please, can't we- I don't know, can't we talk, I'm not-"

He was debating the merits of toppling over the bed to get away when the gauze hit his cheek. For an instant, there was a biting sting and a sharp smell - alcohol? Then the gauze dropped, listless, onto the bed beside him.

Yasmin frowned. Lines pulled at her cheeks when she did, the kind she was too young for. She twitched her pointer finger, and the gauze lifted again. Nicholas very bravely resisted the urge to flinch away, but the moment the gauze touched his skin, it fell.

"What are you doing?" demanded Yasmin.

Nicholas blinked down at the gauze. That was his doing?

"I'm not doing anything," he said dumbly. When he looked back at her, the lines on her face had multiplied, carving out the bridge of her nose and the space between her brows. Nicholas foolishly met her eyes and felt something inside him wither, die, and turn to dust. She wanted to crucify him. "I swear," he added in a rush. "I don't have any magic. I don't know how that happened."

He could've sworn she started to glow. "Do you think you are in any position to play games?"

"No! No games, I hate games-"

"This is not my fucking job, I will not be toyed with-"

"No toys, never toys-"

Nicholas watched in horror as the tips of her hair began to rise in serpentine locks, floating around her head like she was about to turn him to stone. She was glowing, a faint red that haloed her entire body and burned from her eyes. The lamp on the counter flickered wildly, plunging the room back and forth between darkness and light, before surging in size, bursting from the lamp's opening.

Nicholas couldn't believe his last thought was going to be, she shouldn't have the magic to do that.

Instead of death came a pained grunt, not from Nicholas, but from just beyond the cracked doorway. The illusion vanished. Yasmin's hair fell back around her shoulders, the halo disappeared, and the lamp dimmed to a warm glow.

If she had looked homicidal before, she was downright bloodthirsty now. Nicholas thanked whatever higher power existed in this world that her bloodlust was directed at the slowly opening door.

"Quit messing around," she hissed.

A curly head of hair butted through, bearing a pained smirk. "You know I like to put on a show. And why do you always have to go for the groi-"

"I locked the door for a reason. Leave."

The door opened further, revealing a young man with thick eyebrows and brown skin. He came in hunched over, holding his gut like he'd been struck, but when he straightened, he loomed over Yasmin by nearly a head. When had Nicholas made them all so tall?

"I just wanted to greet your patient," said Cairo, counselor to the king. His pout faltered, quivering against a snicker. "Lighten up, doc."

"Leave."

Cairo didn't show any sign he'd heard. His attention had snagged on Nicholas. He skirted around Yasmin to approach with his hands clasped behind his back, bending at the waist and tilting his head left and right like he was observing a trapped animal, or maybe a lab specimen. His face was kinder than Yasmin's but just as unsettling. Nicholas couldn't shake the feeling he was going to be dissected.

"You look normal," Cairo said eventually. He was pouting again. He had a soft, young face that wore it well, but it looked out of place when he stood - someone so large had no right to pout. "Why do you look so normal?"

"...Sorry?"

"He isn't normal," said Yasmin. "He uses strange magic."

"I don't-"

"Hmm, yes, I did see that. Mind if I try?"

"I mind that you're here at all."

Cairo ignored her, beckoning with two fingers to the gauze lying limp on Nicholas' lap, humming when it touched his face and fell right back down.

"That is strange. How'd you do that?"

"I didn't."

"You don't say a whole lot, huh?" Cairo chuckled. "Come closer."

Nocholas obeyed, scooting forward until his legs hung off the bed. Cairo lifted the gauze again, this time with his fingers, and Nicholas hissed at the burn of the alcohol against the cuts in his cheek. Cairo studied him keenly as he cleaned crusted blood from the wound. When he was satisfied, he dropped the dirty gauze onto Nicholas' lap.

Nicholas contemplated the sterility of the gauze after so many falls, and how clean Cairo's hands were. Then he contemplated why a counselor and bodyguard to the king were tending his wounds in a castle infirmary devoid of nurses.

"Did you search him?" Cairo asked Yasmin.

"Of course I searched him."

"I don't know..." he sang, pursing his lips. "Sure doesn't look like you searched him."

A scalpel shot from the cabinet, aimed directly at his throat. Nicholas jumped so hard he nearly fell off the bed, but Cairo barely moved except for the flick of his pointer finger. The scalpel redirected upward and lodged in the ceiling.

"Take off your shirt," Yasmin said to Nicholas like she hadn't just tried to end her comrade.

"Excuse me?" Nicholas squeaked. He saw that twitch reappear in her left eye and scrambled out of his shirt, leaving it in a gray pile next to him.

"Both of them."

Nicholas cringed as he pulled away his undershirt. It clung to his skin. He could say with certainty that he had never known true vulnerability until this very moment, sitting shirtless as two of the strongest mages in Caldora circled his infirmary bed with eyes roaming intently over his chest and arms.

It dawned on him that they were looking for arm cuffs. Like the rings on their fingers, the armlets worn by the Interran people carried minerals that concentrated and channeled their inherent magic. As a non-magical, non-Interran, non-spy, Nicholas was just very naked.

"Nothing," said Yasmin. She looked livid. Cairo looked thrilled. "Get His Majesty."

Nicholas thought very rarely about God, and even less often about faith, but in that moment, he closed his eyes and said a prayer that would bring a priest to tears.

"Yes, darling!" Cairo cackled, turning away with a flourish. Before he slipped back out, he blew Yasmin a kiss. It floated through the air, a tiny red heart-shaped light that she dodged with an animalistic snarl. Another scalpel whizzed through the closing door. Nicholas heard it wedge into the ceiling outside.

Yasmin stood extremely still as she waited, poised with her hands behind her back and a certain strength in her legs, in her stance, like she was ready to hop into combat at any moment. Nicholas, for his part, folded his hands awkwardly over his lap and fidgeted with his posture. Was he supposed to bow when Rayan entered? Or was that too sudden a movement? He didn't like his chances if Yasmin went for another scalpel.

She glanced at him. Her face contorted in honestly hurtful levels of disdain. "Dress yourself before the king arrives."

Nicholas was still on the last button of his shirt when he heard the telltale heavy footsteps. He had opted out of putting his sweat-stained undershirt back on; he hurried to force it into a crumpled ball and sat on top of it right as the door opened. Yasmin dropped into a deep bow and didn't rise until King Rayan strode past her, Cairo on his heels. Nicholas hastened to follow her lead, then remembered his bad ankle and the disgusting shirt under his ass and ended up performing a weird aborted hop in place on the bed. Cairo raised an eyebrow. Behind him, Yasmin sighed. Nicholas bent at the neck in a sad excuse for a bow.

"Yo-" His voice cracked. "Your Majesty."

"Raise your head."

It was a trap. Nicholas lifted his chin and was at once shackled in place, powerless to look away. Not because he didn't want to - it went against everything he'd ever learned about survival, looking a wild beast dead in the eye - but Rayan was giving an order, so potent it didn't need to be spoken aloud. Look at me. It was imperial, narcissistic, in every way befitting a king. It said, try and lie to me now.

A square bandage floated toward him. Nicholas couldn't see any movement of Rayan's hand, but he could see the blue glow of his ring. The bandage touched Nicholas' skin and went limp. Rayan considered him for a long moment, and Nicholas sat motionless, hardly even breathing.

A gloved finger touched his cheek, pushing his face to one side. Then, without preamble, Rayan lit a fire in his hand.

Nicholas didn't even have time to react. A cruel gust of heat brushed his wound and stung his eye for a split second as the flame bloomed, and then-nothing. Nicholas jolted too late, a second after the damage should have been dealt, but in place of scorching pain he felt cool silk against his skin. It hurt, but only because the wound was so tender.

"I'll give you this," said Rayan. "You put on a very convincing show."

"Wait..." Nicholas started to say. He had nothing to follow it with, caught up in a disorienting inner clash - the blinding relief that the flame hadn't touched him, pitted against the grim awareness that he might have been better off if it did.

The king said to his most trusted men, "That settles it, then."

"Wait," Nicholas tried again, but Rayan had given him his back.

"We must act without delay," said Yasmin. The three of them stood in a triangle, wholly blocking him out.

"I must act carefully."

Yasmin bristled. "How long will you turn a blind eye? You leave your kingdom at Interra's mercy."

"I have nothing to do with Interra," Nicholas swore. Yasmin talked right over him.

"We're sitting ducks if Adrian has somehow found a way to nullify our magic!"

"No, that's not-"

"Do not forget your station," Rayan warned. Cairo looked back and forth between them, blatantly delighted.

"What is it you suggest, then?" said Yasmin. "You've already given him more mercy than he deserves."

"Execution!" Cairo supplied cheerily.

"Please, just let me-"

"You will unearth the source of his magic," said Rayan. "Through whatever means necessary."

"I don't have any magic-"

"Stoop as low as you must. I have run out of grace."

"Listen to me!"

Three pairs of eyes shot to Nicholas. For a moment, he only stared back, shocked by the sound of his own voice. He couldn't remember the last time he'd shouted. He was routinely spoken over, and he did not force himself to be heard. It scratched his throat. His hand came over his mouth belatedly, like he might somehow catch his outburst and push it back down his windpipe.

"Oho?" Cairo poked his head over Rayan's shoulder, grinning wide.

For a man so intentionally expressionless, it turned out that the king did not hide surprise well. It showed in the slight jump to his shoulder, like no one had ever raised their voice at him before (oh god, maybe no one had), and the jerky way he turned to Nicholas.

"I am so sorry," Nicholas blurted. He bowed as much as his position allowed. "I shouldn't have-"

"You won my attention," Rayan said coolly. A lock of hair slipped out of the tie at the base of his skull as he angled his head downward. "Do not waste it."

Nicholas slowly sat up. He shoved down whatever had surged out of him and reverted back to the rules, born of observation, that had governed most of his interactions up until this point. Pick your words carefully, don't say too much. Talk for too long and they'll stop listening.

"I was born in South Simona to a Caldoran tradesman." Straightforward, concise, carefully neutral. He had been perfecting this for years. "I don't have any ties to Interra."

On the map Nicholas had drawn some ten pages into the journal, South Simona was the second largest city in Caldora and the closest to the frontier.

"Simona, you say," pondered Rayan. "Then I should find some record of you and this tradesman there, yes?"

"He died along with my mom when I was young," said Nicholas. This, at least, he knew was convincing, spoken with the colorless sober conviction only someone who had lived it could wield. He held fast to the king's gaze and let him look as deep as he wished, challenging him to find a lie that was not there. "Not sure how well-kept the orphan records are."

"I suppose you'll tell me there isn't anyone around who can vouch for you, either?"

"I tend to keep to myself."

Rayan reached into his coat and came out with Nicholas' phone. It was cracked so badly he doubted it would ever light up again. "I can't say I've seen such a device in Simona. Or anywhere in Caldora, for that matter."

"My dad collected lots of weird foreign items on his travels."

"Such as these?" This time, Rayan retrieved Nicholas' wallet, flipping it open to reveal his array of credit cards and a whopping four dollar bills. "Oh. Is this the tradesman in question?"

In the clear pocket was a photo of a seven-year-old Nicholas squished between his parents' beaming smiles, red in the face, scowling wistfully off-camera at the students on the playground while his mom held up the plastic gold medal he'd won in a picture book competition. Nicholas reached out without thinking. Rayan moved the wallet away and studied it.

"This image is so lifelike," he mused.

Nicholas knew the feeling of being played with and handled it well enough - he had dealt with mean-spirited classmates and condescending professors and Ava fucking Dubois - but even the lowest of people had never stooped to his family. "Realism has come a long way," he said through his teeth.

Rayan pocketed the wallet and the phone. "What else did your father leave behind for you?"

"Everything burned right along with him in the fire."

The slightest downturn pulled at one corner of the king's mouth. Nicholas had a feeling they were thinking the same thing: tracking down documentation of a single orphan or a decade-old house fire in a huge urban center like Simona would be nearly impossible.

"And your clothing?" the king pressed. He leaned forward, forcing Nicholas to lift his chin to keep meeting that unspoken demand, look at me. It was a calculated, smug move, meant to intimidate. And it did. Nicholas was sweating through his second shirt. But he was fucking peeved, too.

"It's not so different from yours," he said. "A more current fashion, maybe. Must take a while for trends to get all the way here."

He had to fight off a full-body cringe at his own words, just this side of snarky. It was unlike him to be easily provoked. He cursed his mundane life for dulling his survival instincts to the point that he would test the king of mages, of all people. He was not himself, and he blamed it on the hungry ache in his stomach and the pain he felt all over. God, when was the last time he'd slept?

"You're quick," said Rayan. "What explanation do you have for the book? Please, I'd love to hear it."

Nicholas was losing ground. He curled his fingers into the thin sheet but he could feel himself slipping. He tried his best to hide it. Straightforward, concise, carefully neutral. "I'm a writer. It's fiction."

"Fiction in which you've drawn my death at the hands of the next Interran king."

"My- my art is not a reflection of my beliefs."

"So you don't think I'm...what did it say? I think cold, domineering, and detached from my people were on the list?"

Nicholas swallowed. "No, sir."

"And what of your sudden appearance in North Simona? Your strange magic?"

"I don't have any-"

The small flame in the lamp exploded. Glass shattered over the counter, showering the floor alongside dying embers as the room went dark. "Then what do you call it?" the king finally snapped.

Straightforward, concise-

"I don't know! I don't know, I don't know, you hate that I don't know but it's the only answer I have!"

He couldn't do it anymore. His body felt so heavy. He teetered forward, unsteady, finding the king's eyes in the darkness even as everything gushed to the surface. All the anger and all the aching, the paralyzing fear that there was no way out of this. "I swear on my life I am the most confused person here, you can keep hurting me all you want but I have nothing to give you, I just- I need help."

Nicholas wondered what he was doing, begging a merciless man for pity. He wondered if he would die here. The sad truth, the one he'd hoped to one day change with his novel, was that no one would notice his absence. There was something ironic in that. He didn't have the energy to think about it.

"Treat his wounds," said Rayan.

Light spilled in as the door opened, but he turned before Nicholas could see his face.

"Sir!" Yasmin cried, outraged. The door slammed in her face.

4. Speak

Humming under his breath, Cairo knelt to wrap Nicholas' ankle where it dangled off the side of the infirmary bed. He was none too careful about it. Nicholas clutched the sheets, breathing deep and doing his best not to wince. He had a bad feeling Cairo was the sadistic type to jostle his foot even more if he realized how much pain he was in. By "had a bad feeling," of course, he meant he knew without a doubt, because he had written Cairo to be exactly that type.

"Exceptional," Cairo marveled when he was done, beaming up at Nicholas. "I really put you through the ringer there, and still, not a word. I can't tell whether to be bored or impressed."

Okay, so. Even more sadistic he'd thought. The relief Nicholas had felt when Yasmin stormed out of the infirmary after Rayan was starting to seem premature.

"I'm just grateful that you're helping me."

Cairo laughed. "Buttering me up! What do I have to do to get you going like you were a minute ago?"

"I, um. What?"

"With the king!" He puffed out his chest and raised his chin to leer up at Nicholas. "Foolish king, look at you! Look at your clothes! You cannot even keep up with fashion, and yet you think you can keep up with my mind games? You will never know my secrets!"

Nicholas blanched. Was that what they'd heard? "I...don't remember saying that."

"I wish you would've!" Cairo hopped to his feet. He grabbed the bandage Rayan had left on the bed and slapped it onto Nicholas' cheek, laughing again when Nicholas hissed. Suddenly, he leaned over the bed, bent practically in half to reach his eye level. "Secrets, secrets," he said. "How many do you think you have, just off the top of your head?"

"...None."

"The fundamental human lie, so often told and so rarely believed. Humor me. How many?"

"I-" Nicholas cleared his throat. He was reaching his interrogation quota for the day. "I don't know."

"Fine then, just name a few. Tell me a secret, little spy."

"I'm not a spy."

"No, no, that's not a secret, that's another lie." Cairo tipped into his space, like he might find what he wanted written along the vessels in Nicholas' eyes. Nicholas edged back just enough to breathe his own air (and maybe he was a bit scared that Cairo would find what he was looking for), then some more when Cairo leaned even closer. There was a playful flash in Cairo's eye just before Nicholas went too far and lost the fight with gravity, flailing to catch himself on his wrists.

"Kidding, kidding!" Cairo beckoned at the air, and the blindfold dropped itself into his palm. He reached around Nicholas' head and tied it over his eyes, giggling all the way. "I'm sure you're very innocent. More importantly, though, you are very, very gross."

Thanks, Nicholas thought.

"You should be hanged for facing the king in such a state!"

And with that, his arms finally gave out and he dropped flat onto his back on the bed. Cairo howled with laughter. "Kidding again! You're very funny, you know, for someone boring."

Nicholas stayed where he was, laid out sideways on the bed, and thought that he might have been better off with Yasmin. He jumped when Cairo took both of his hands. A metal cuff locked around one of his wrists, then the other. He was hauled out of the bed without warning.

"Are you ready?"

"For what?"

"Splendid. Let's go."

He wasn't any more considerate of Nicholas' foot than Yasmin had been. He dragged him down winding torchlit halls with a skip in his step, singing the same song he had been humming earlier. He didn't know many of the words, so it was mostly nonsensical lyrics and unnecessary runs. He kept inviting Nicholas to sing along. Each time, Nicholas would exaggerate a wince and pretend he was too caught up in the pain in his foot to hear.

He feared the worst - surely there had to be a torture chamber somewhere in this castle - but the blindfold was swiped from his face in a bathroom. The half-filled square tub at the center was the size of his bed back home. Behind it, rosy curtains glowed with early dawn light. Nicholas grimaced when he glimpsed himself in a standing mirror, but the image checked out: greasy skin, sweat stains, vaguely ghoulish complexion. Purple-red bruising stained most of the left half of his face and his mouth was caked with dried blood.

Cairo appeared behind him in the reflection. Nicholas had never thought himself particularly short until that moment. "Hm. Yes, you look terrible."

Thanks, Nicholas thought again.

Cairo made a grand sweeping gesture toward the bath. He was holding a bar of soap. "Come on, now."

Nicholas met his eye in the mirror, then looked at the bath, then met his eye again.

"I can, you know. Bathe myself."

"Very well."

Cairo remained where he was, watching Nicholas expectantly.

"So are you staying, or...?"

"Yaz abandoned post, so it falls on me to act as your keeper."

"Right, but..." Did he have to act as keeper from inside the bathroom?

"Oh! You're modest." Cairo turned his back and took a couple of steps toward the opposite wall. It didn't put him any closer to the door. Nicholas, a seasoned professional at picking his battles, began to undress.

The bathwater was cold. He lowered himself clumsily, stiff from the chill and only mostly managing to keep his foot dry. Propping it awkwardly at the edge of the tub, he took a deep breath, braced himself, and slid down the mosaic tiles until he was submerged.

It was freezing, and he was seriously pushing the limits of his flexibility, but everything was quiet the moment the water closed over his head. All the white noise he hadn't noticed - the early morning birdsong outside, the shuffling of the waking castle, Cairo's footsteps meters away - got trapped above the surface. The cold water eased his heartbeat, soothed his broken skin, and pressed like a blanket around his head until even his mind slowed down.

His tub at home was barely big enough to shower in, let alone bathe, and his apartment didn't have a pool. It had been a while. He had forgotten how much he needed this.

He didn't know how long he stayed like that. Too long, probably. Not long enough after everything he'd been through. His lungs burned, and he emerged gasping.

"Oh, good. I thought you might've died," Cairo said without inflection. "You've ruined your bandage."

Nicholas followed his eyeline to where it floated in the water. Right by his hip. He covered his crotch with his hands. "Right, right, carry on," Cairo said, turning around.

The bar of soap was on the washstand. Nicholas regretted getting in the bath without grabbing it as he stretched as far as his body would allow and barely grazed it with his fingertips. He slipped, sending water splashing and knocking the pitcher with his knuckles. "Shit," he mumbled, helpless to do anything but wince as porcelain went diving to the floor.

It stopped inches above the patterned tile and glided back onto the washstand. When it landed, it pushed the soap just within Nicholas' reach. The whole thing made him question how much privacy he was really getting.

He scrubbed his skin vigorously everywhere it didn't hurt and delicately everywhere it did. His hair was a nightmare; he wished he would've known to cut it shorter before getting sucked into a magical journal. By the time he sank beneath the surface again, he could see the sunrise in the gap between the curtains. He rinsed his hair, then emerged.

He only made it out to his nose before a force clamped down on his shoulder. A stream of bubbles jumped to the surface as his yelp was silenced by the water. Nicholas struggled against the hold, but he had very little leverage, and Cairo was stronger than he looked.

"You're shivering," Cairo said next to his ear.

His other hand dipped into the bath. In seconds, it was steaming. It burned the sores on Nicholas' torso and the cut on his cheek; he gasped and got a lungful of hot water. Scrabbling at the sides of the tub, he tilted his chin up for air and coughed up suds. Cairo let up enough so he could breathe but didn't budge as Nicholas lurched upward with all his strength, an immovable force trapping him in the scorching water.

"My king is generous to a fault," said Cairo. There was no strain in his voice though Nicholas thrashed in his hold. "It would be nasty to take advantage of that. Don't you agree?"

"Yes," Nicholas wheezed.

"Hm?"

He cried, "Yes!"

"If you really are a spy-"

"I'm not! I'm not, I'm not-"

Nicholas was pushed under. His tongue, his cheek, his eyelids, his nose- all of it burned.

Cairo dragged him out by the hair. "Do not interrupt me." Nicholas folded forward, hacking, only to be yanked back. "The minute you so much as scratch his skin will be your last. Do you understand?"

"I understand," Nicholas panted. "I understand."

"Delightful." Cairo released him.

Nicholas hauled his upper body out of the water and stayed there until his lungs cleared, braced on shaking arms and a busted leg. By the time he clambered all the way out, Cairo was humming that same song with his back turned. A towel hovered over Nicholas and dropped onto his head.

White pants and a linen shirt were folded over the edge of the tub. Wet spots dotted the soft material. It should have been too hot in the steaming room, but Nicholas was shivering all over.

"We should probably replace that bandage, yeah?" said Cairo. A pair of sandals waited by the washstand.

□ □ □

Daylight spilled beneath the divider into his little section of the infirmary. Nicholas eyed it and wondered how long he'd been awake. He was nestled in the sheets, completely alone and more tired than he'd ever been, but he couldn't sleep.

Someone was at the door. He heard the lock give and prepared himself for Cairo with a deep breath that left him in a sputtering mess when the king walked in instead. Nicholas hastened upright and into another shitty half-bow.

"You're surprised," Rayan observed. A tray floated into the room behind him, bringing a sweet scent with it. Unsure how else to respond, Nicholas nodded. "Cairo has duties to attend to. He cannot waste an entire day posted in front of your door."

Another nod. Don't you have guards for that? Nicholas didn't say. The tray settled over his lap. There was a large bowl of oatmeal and a glass of water. And servants for this?

It was hardly a glamorous meal. His tongue pooled with saliva anyway. He hesitated, breathing through his mouth to avoid the smell of cinnamon.

"You may eat in my presence."

The king waited. Nicholas' stomach gave a sad groan.

"If I wanted to kill you, I would not need poison to do it."

Nicholas couldn't argue with that and didn't really want to. With the hand that wasn't cuffed to the bed, he spooned a heaping bite of oatmeal and chugged the glass. The king didn't speak or move until the bowl was clean. His silence was even more brutal than Yasmin's. It carried none of her anger, but Nicholas swallowed each mouthful with the uncomfortable awareness that he was being scrutinized. What Rayan hoped to glean from his chewing habits, he couldn't say.

He approached the bed as soon as Nicholas was done. A stool from somewhere deeper in the room nestled itself at the bedside, and the king settled on it.

"You claim to have no magic," he said. "Is that the story you're sticking to?"

"It's the truth."

Rayan waved his hand. A large flat box fell onto his palm. It was simple on the outside, wrapped in navy silk and secured with a lock. He set it at the edge of the bed.

"Turn over your hand," he ordered off-handedly, popping open the top. The box's contents faced away from Nicholas. Rayan took out a dark, raw gemstone the size of his palm that glinted blue from the right angle. If it weren't for the ring on his pointer finger, cut and polished but glowing the same icy blue when he sent the tray drifting onto the counter, Nicholas wouldn't have caught on: the rock Rayan deposited wordlessly into Nicholas' open palm was forcate, the mineral that granted mages like him, Yasmin, and Cairo control over mass and its movement.

Rayan slipped off his right glove. Nicholas inhaled sharply through his nose when two fingers laid over his pulse point. He glanced up from the touch on his wrist, bewildered, to find Rayan already watching him. There it was again, that quiet look at me.

It was harder this time, with cold fingers on Nicholas' skin and no way of knowing what he was being tested on. Rayan put the gemstone away without explaining, and Nicholas wondered if this was something he was expected to understand as a born-and-raised Caldoran, or if the king was just being an asshole.

Another rock was placed on his palm. This one was tinted faintly red - vigalis. Energy transformation, light and fire. When Rayan touched Nicholas' wrist again, his knuckles brushed the gemstone, and for the second the contact lasted there was a faint pulse in his fingertips, thrumming against Nicholas' veins. Rayan shifted his hand so he wasn't touching the stone and the feeling left.

Ah, Nicholas understood. So that's what he's looking for.

This was a test he could pass with flying colors.

"If there's something you'd like to say," said Rayan, "Just say it."

Nicholas startled. His expression couldn't have changed much, yet Rayan had read the question on his tongue. It was unnerving to be under such careful attention.

The stone felt warmer in his palm than it had a second ago. The king took it back and the warmth vanished, and Nicholas thought he must have imagined it. "When you confirm that I have no magic, will you let me go?" he asked.

Rayan let out a short, low puff of air that might have been a laugh. "Nico, Nico," he tsked. Something twitched in Nicholas' cheek. Rayan zeroed in on it. "Something on your mind?"

There was nothing in his inflection or on his face to suggest he was goading, but Nicholas heard it all the same. He didn't take the bait. A jagged black gemstone settled in his hand, glimmering gold when the light hit it: encaline, the charmstone.

"You won't be punished for speaking your mind," said Rayan. "So speak."

It sounded like a trap. But it also sounded like an order. Lose-lose. "My name is Nicholas."

"I see."

It happened again, the warmth. The encaline grew hotter with every second it sat in Nicholas' hand. He panicked for a moment, but Rayan didn't show any sign that he could feel a reaction under his skin.

"Afraid?" said Rayan. "What of?"

"You." It was the first front that came to mind, and it was at least a little true. Nicholas schooled his expression even as the heat started to bite at his skin. Rayan broke eye contact for the first time, diverting his attention as he took the encaline - it didn't seem to burn him - but Nicholas caught the way his mouth twitched. A smile, maybe, if he was capable of that sort of thing. "Poor Nico."

Irritation flared in Nicholas' chest. Between the king and his men, Rayan was the only one yet to lay a hand on him, but Nicholas thought he might prefer Yasmin's fury and Cairo's crazy over- this. This vain, patronizing game Rayan seemed to be playing. The others were rougher, but at least they didn't make Nicholas want to say something that would actually land him in a torture chamber.

"Speak," the king said again. Nicholas hated this, being read so easily. Nobody had ever looked so close before. A round stone streaked with violet bands was pressed to his tingling palm. Nicholas recognized it as inercium, a mineral that commanded matter in state and form.

"I..." He chewed his bottom lip. He watched Rayan's eyes, tried to read him right back, but the king's face was blank. He thought, though, that despite his god-awful personality, Rayan had a decisive honesty to him. Not because he was kind, but because a man of his station had no reason to lie. He had said Nicholas could speak his mind, and Nicholas- he didn't like him, was starting to think maybe he couldn't stand him, but he believed him. "I never said you could call me that."

Rayan tilted his head. "Do I seem to you like a man who asks for permission?"

Yeah. Nicholas couldn't stand him.

The inercium was replaced with a metallic indigo slab. Tomite, the fifth and final Caldoran mineral, was among the hardest to master, but those who did could manipulate matter at the molecular level.

Rayan and Cairo were rare cases of Caldorans that wielded all five minerals. Most mages could use two or three at best, and most citizens couldn't use any at all. It was a matter of birth and probably breeding.

Nicholas thought it would be over after that, but Rayan procured another stone. It was lighter than the others, a pale yellow crystal that felt dusty against his skin. This was an Interran life stone.

"Perplexed," Rayan noted. Nicholas' nose scrunched, just barely. "Irritated."

"Are you having fun?" Nicholas deadpanned, then pressed his lips together, instantly regretful. What happened to biting your tongue? He was good at biting his tongue. An expert, even. But it kept slipping around Rayan, and he didn't know why, and it wasn't a mistake he could afford.

"Ah," said Rayan. "There it is."

Nicholas felt his jaw clench and immediately relaxed before Rayan could latch onto it. He didn't know what the king was getting from this, but he wouldn't willfully be his entertainment unless it was going to get him out of here.

Another mineral, also from Interra, replaced the last. It was heavy, flat, and mossy green - earth. Next, a chunk of geode with steely blue crystals - water - and after that, a smooth orange stone - growth. Nicholas hadn't expected its opal sheen. Rayan lingered over this last one so long it started to prickle with heat.

"So you truly are powerless," he said. He didn't lift his fingers or the stone.

"Doesn't this mean you can let me leave?" Nicholas tried again. "I'm not a threat to you."

"Is that so? You cannot use magic, but it cannot be used against you, either. That alone makes you a threat."

Nicholas' palm was stinging now. He didn't let it show on his face, not even when it started to burn. The last thing he needed was to give Rayan something else to study. He couldn't quite keep it from his voice, though; his words were rushed and tinged with desperation. "I just want to go home."

The veins in his wrist bulged with the effort to resist dropping the stone when the heat became unbearable. Focused on his face, Rayan didn't notice. He tapped his fingers absentmindedly against Nicholas' wrist and said, "I don't really care."

Nicholas was too worried about his face and the pain he couldn't show to think over his words. "You're not very kind," he said without the presence of mind to hesitate, but Rayan didn't seem offended. He might've even been smiling again, lips parted around an unspoken word. Nicholas could guess what it had been, the interrupted command that had him looking so self-satisfied. Speak.

"No." Rayan finally took away the last stone, and Nicholas curled his fingers before the blisters on his palm could catch the light. Pulling his glove back over his hand, the king stood to leave. "I suppose I'm not."

5. Pot and Kettle

When he was finally allowed to sleep, Nicholas dreamed of Eden.

It was strange– he hadn't been to this place before, this effusive garden, but he knew at the first stroke of green against his mindspace that it was holy.

It was strange– he hadn't seen the start of the world, but something here was familiar, something in the opalescent surface of the still pond. Was that mist rising from it, or was it boiling? He stretched out a hand to check and found his arm did not exist; he was not here. This was not his story.

It was strange– he hadn't been religious since his parents went up in flames, but he thought he remembered a river in Genesis, not a pond. One river, four headwaters, and two great trees. This was not the garden of Eden.

If this wasn't Eden, then the pair dancing between the oleander bushes wasn't Adam and Eve. The more he observed, the more foolish he felt for even considering it. They were too clothed, and too lewd when they moved together. They couldn't possibly be ignorant.

What would poisonous flowers be doing in paradise, anyway?

Still, they felt bigger than the earth they roamed. Like they existed to mark the start of something, or the end.

In a heartbeat, the woman was before him, or not-him, or whatever he was. She was beautiful in the watery light, and she was terrifying, and she was anything but holy. He had seen her before. Torrents of dark hair fell over her shoulder with the tilt of her head. She had a long neck and a sharp collar, naked and bruised where her lover had pulled down her shirt to mark it. She could nearly be called curious, if not for the black wells within her irises that seemed to already know everything. Her partner danced on, so naive Nicholas could've been convinced he really was Adam if not for the silk robes on his back.

"You are not supposed to be here," she said in a deep, echoing voice too large for her narrow chest. When she spoke again, Nicholas realized it wasn't coming from her chest at all. "So we're doing the impossible now, are we?"

Her words seemed to float off from the pond with the mist– no, steam– no, smoke. The air was turning black with it. Her skin, too. First a small spot at the center of her chest, then a blotch on her cheek, then her fingertips. Patches of necrotic skin spread and started to burn, peeling away at their inception, ember-red at the edges like she was made of paper. The flora around the pond wilted, from the moss hugging the stones to the topmost leaves. Everything except the oleander.

A cry rang out, laden with an anguish so deep Nicholas wished to cover his ears, if only he had any. Her lover raced for her as her hair caught flame, but he was wilting, too (and he seemed more familiar that way), until he was just loose skin sagging over a skeletal frame.

"I didn't think that was allowed, anymore," the woman said. Her lover's hand, now nothing but bone, landed on her shoulder. She reached up to hold it just as her fingers turned to ash, and his to dust. She seemed timelessly sad. "Well, anyway. Welcome."

Nicholas could smell the smoke.

He breathed it in, relieved to have his faculties back. If he had his voice, too, he could ask her for help. She would know how to get him home; she knew everything. But he breathed in too long, and smoke coated his lungs until he was coughing.

He shot upright. It tasted foul and burned his throat. He searched for a source through teary eyes and saw gray-black curling in through the gap under the infirmary door.

His hearing came back to him last, and with it an overwhelming surge of noise. Crashing, breaking, shouting. The crackling of flames was loud and close, right outside his door.

"Fuck," he choked. A window– there was a window on the other side of the infirmary. Its daylight crawled along the floor, beneath the divider. He surged from the bed, or tried too. A punching pain spiked in his left shoulder as his arm pulled taught, bound at the wrist to the bed.

The whole room was hot, so hot his skin was slick with sweat, but he suddenly felt very, very cold.

He was trapped.

He pulled until his wrist was raw, but the cuff and the bed frame were both metal. Desperate, he clambered out of the bed, numb to the twinge in his ankle, to heave with his entire body, clenching his fingers together like he might somehow squeeze through a cuff hardly wider than his wrist.

His breath came in ragged pants broken up by fits of coughing, until a gray haze hung across the whole room and cough was all he could do. He dropped to his knees and keeled forward and managed a clear inhale through his nose. Sweat and smoke stung his eyes. He was vaguely aware of blood dripping over his knuckles. He kept thrashing against the cuffs anyway, and he didn't shout for help.

The king would probably be thrilled if a tragic accident took him. No point wasting what little clear air he had left.

Distantly, he heard an outraged shout – "Sir!" – right before the door burst open. Flames surged into the room, bringing with them oppressive heat. What a miserable way to go, Nicholas thought, but they hardly got past the door before curling into themselves, retreating like they'd been suctioned out. In their place appeared a person, one he almost didn't recognize at first glance.

Rayan's eyes were frantic as he rushed into the room. They zeroed in on Nicholas, and in an instant he was crouched at the bedside.

"Shit," he muttered when he took in Nicholas' state and the handcuffs trapping him against the bed. Past him, Nicholas could see fire trying to creep into the room, held back as if by an invisible wall. The smoke receded too, wiped away with a sweep of his arm. Nicholas tried to suck in the clean air and wound up choking. "Shit, are you– shit."

Rayan had one hand facing the flames, a flat palm keeping them at bay. The other fumbled over his clothes in search of something. But the king was dressed for sleep, in a white silk shirt and pants. "Shit!"

A gloved hand came down over Nicholas' wrist. Inercium glowed purple as energy hummed beneath Rayan's palm, but it stopped short, and the cuff remained. "Fuck, right– sorry–"

There was an ear-splitting screech. Through the door, Nicholas glimpsed rusty red feathers over an impossibly large form and an arrowhead beak that parted with another cry, spilling fire over the hall outside.

Rayan touched the chain linking the cuffs this time, and they fell apart easily. There was a wounded squawk as the beast in the hallway careened out of view, then a sound like shattering glass. Yasmin appeared in the doorway, face stricken with worry that morphed into an exasperated scowl when she spotted the king.

"Must you insist on making my job so difficult?"

She pressed her palms downward. The floor plunged away beneath them, and Nicholas found himself in free-fall.

The drop was so short that he barely had time to shout. Hands gripped his shoulders hard the instant before he hit the ground, slowing his fall by a fraction of a second. He lashed out on instinct, shoving Rayan back and stumbling away, then barking a curse when he landed too hard on his bad foot.

"I wasn't—" Rayan said breathlessly from somewhere ahead. The room was completely dark. Nicholas couldn't hear his own thoughts over his heart pummeling his lungs, beating out every gasping breath he took. "I was just— your ankle."

Nicholas' back hit the wall. Whatever space they were in, it was small and smelled like earth. So he was trapped in a tight space, probably underground, with a magical villainous king. A magical villainous king he had just shoved.

"Oh god." His body shook with another round of hacking. He rode it out helplessly, clutching his chest. Between the last lingering coughs, he managed, "I am so sorry...I don't...know why—"

"Don't apologize."

Nicholas took hiccuping breaths, forcefully slow, until he managed a full cycle in and out. A flame appeared in Rayan's palm, casting warm orange light. Even up close, he was almost unrecognizable, with color flushing his cheeks and hair falling messily around his face. The longest strands in the back just reached his shoulders. He wore nightclothes even though it had to be mid-day.

It was strange– seeing him like this, picturing him sleeping in until late afternoon. It was a little too human.

At least the gloves were still there, stark against his all-white.

The room they were in wasn't much of a room at all. It was at best a four by four space with nothing in it. The tiles on the floor were the very same as the infirmary, and the stone walls were caked with dirt. The ceiling was too high to make out in the firelight.

"Ask," said Rayan. Nicholas' eyes snapped from the ceiling to his face, but Rayan wasn't messing with him. He couldn't pinpoint exactly how he knew. Now that he'd caught his breath, the king had returned to his careful neutrality, expressionless and inflectionless. It was a far cry from the look on his face when he'd burst into the infirmary. Nicholas could almost believe he'd imagined the wild panic that had blackened Rayan's eyes and the feverish voice that had stuttered curses at his side.

"Where are we?" he asked. He sounded terrible.

Rayan shrugged. "The foundations, if I had to guess. Maybe inside some absurdly thick basement wall. Just...down. You're alright?"

Rayan asked in monotone, but the fact that he asked at all...maybe Nicholas had hit his head during the drop. He was dizzy. And his head hurt from coughing so much, and his wrist felt terrible now that the adrenaline had faded, but he said, "Fine."

"You're bleeding."

"Right. Guess I've been better."

"Why did you do that to your wrist?"

"I was trying to get out."

"You shouldn't have done that."

Nicholas frowned. "I didn't want to just die."

"You would have died anyway. It was unnecessary added pain. Surely you knew it was futile."

"All I knew," Nicholas said evenly, "was that I was going to burn alive because I was handcuffed to a bed." He made a real effort not to snap, but that last part came out caustic.

It met its mark. Rayan didn't counter.

"But...you're right," said Nicholas. "I would have died. So. Thanks."

"Sit. We'll probably be here for a while."

Nicholas slid clumsily down the wall on one foot. Rayan remained as he was, so Nicholas had to crane his neck to see his face. It could have been some sort of power play Nicholas had fallen for, but Rayan wasn't looking down at him at all. He stared at the wall, quiet.

"What's going on?" said Nicholas.

"Attack," Rayan muttered. Nicholas couldn't tell if he was lost in thought or intentionally being difficult. His personal biases leaned toward the latter.

"...Do fire-breathing birds attack your castle often?"

"No. Never."

Rayan's hands clasped at his front. The flame floated before him, lighting his face from below. He fiddled with his rings one after the other – tomite, encaline, vigalis, forcate, and inercium, pinkie to thumb on his left hand. He twisted them around, slid them past his second knuckle and pushed them back down, scraped his thumb against the stones.

There was nothing else to watch, so Nicholas watched him fidget. Rayan had a pianist's hands. For all Nicholas knew, he was a pianist. Maybe that was another decision the journal had made without him. And while it was at it, hopefully the journal had come up with some explanation as to why Rayan wore gloves under his rings. It never occurred to Nicholas how odd that was until he stared at it for minutes.

The king was antsy, and doing a surprisingly bad job at hiding it. He was fully taking off his rings now, removing all four before shoving them back on and repeating.

"What is it."

Nicholas raised his head and found Rayan looking at him. "What?"

"Your question. What is it."

"How do you do that?" It hadn't been the question on his mind, but it was now. Rayan's weird little game wouldn't be so bothersome if he wasn't so good at it. "It's like you're reading my mind."

"I can't read minds."

"I know, I know."

"If I could, I wouldn't ask."

"I know, but I don't understand how you...I'm not very expressive. I'm not."

He had been told as much enough times to believe it. Five months into his move from Washington to Montanna, his fourth grade teacher had leaned across her desk to tell his Uncle Sam in that soft, cloying voice adults used because they thought children wouldn't understand the words if they were spoken sweetly enough: There is an apathy to him like I've never seen. He's traumatized, isn't he. Yeah, mm, yeah, thought so. Do you know how hard it is to find an apathetic nine-year-old?

The kids in his middle school homeroom had called him a robot – all three years, a different class each year. His boyfriend had called him a colorless, emotionally-stunted caricature of a human, roughly thirteen months after their first kiss and precisely nine minutes before their end.

"You're not expressionless, either," said Rayan. "You are...how should I say. Deeply fucking repressed."

Nicholas considered Rayan, in all of his calculated detachment, and thought, you, too.

"Did someone tell you otherwise? They weren't looking close enough."

"And why are you looking so close?" said Nicholas. He added, "Sir."

"I'm trying to figure out whether you want me dead."

Right. Naturally. Because Nicholas was allegedly an Interran spy.

"And I don't often find a worthwhile challenge."

Right, naturally. Because Rayan was most definitely an entitled prick.

Nicholas pointedly lowered his gaze to where Rayan was still messing with his rings and said, "Restless."

The king's brows furrowed for a short second, so slightly Nicholas wouldn't have seen it if the fire didn't cast such drastic shadows over his face– "Confused" –before rising. "Surprised. Maybe a little impressed."

Rayan looked at him for so long, Nicholas had time to not only think about his own actions but make a mental list of their possible consequences. Unsurprisingly, choosing to mock the magical villainous king he was stuck underground with yielded a very grave list of outcomes.

Nowhere on that list did Rayan crack a startled smile and say, "Well played, Nico." It was gone as quickly as it came.

He sat down with his back to the wall opposite Nicholas. His legs took up a ridiculous amount of space. "Was that your only question?" he asked. It wasn't, and it bothered Nicholas to no end that he could tell.

"You could fight that thing," Nicholas said. "Probably better than anyone up there. So why...?"

Yasmin couldn't control fire. Cairo had vigalis, but it wasn't his strongest, and he was the worst fighter of the three of them. That wasn't to say he was weak – just that Rayan was very strong, and Yasmin was the only person skilled enough to protect him. Out of all the talented nobles and castle guards, Nicholas was fairly confident Rayan was the best suited to take on a fire-breathing bird.

Rayan tipped his head back, looking up as though he might see through the ceiling to the fight above. He cracked each one of his knuckles. Nicholas hated that sound. But it was telling; the king was agitated. With Nicholas' question, or maybe with the situation – with the fact that he was so far removed from the fight, the only thing he could hear was the echo of his own knuckles popping.

"Yasmin takes her position very seriously," he said. "That is why I hired her."

He could easily leave the room if he wanted to. And he clearly wanted to. Was it respect for Yasmin, then, that kept him here? Nicholas hadn't thought Rayan respected anyone. He wasn't...supposed to.

What was it Cici had said? You don't know your characters very well.

"You think so loudly," said the king. "It's irritating."

Nicholas didn't know what he was supposed to do about that. Was he meant to stop thinking just because His Majesty was uncomfortable? "Sorry."

He had long since accepted his place in the margins, and he didn't mind – he didn't – because when all was said and done, he could escape into himself. His head had always been the one place he could talk freely. Rayan's attention felt like an invasion of his sacred space. Here, especially, it made Nicholas claustrophobic.

"No need to get so angry," Rayan said dismissively. "You'd be less frustrating if you said what was on your mind, is all."

"I'm," Nicholas began, but he came to a sluggish, bemused stop. He didn't have a response for this, for being asked to talk more. It wasn't something people wanted from him often. "Not that kind of guy," he finished lamely.

"I don't believe you," said Rayan. "It amazes me that you've gotten away with that guise for so long."

Before Nicholas could even try to process that (and maybe it was for the best, because what the hell was he supposed to take from that?), the ceiling opened up with a deep scrape. Two figures crouched over the edge to look down at them.

"All clear!" shouted Cairo. Aside from a smudge of ash across his cheek, he looked normal. Yasmin, on the other hand, had soot streaked across her face. It really added to the effect when she glared at him. "Sorry, I got excited. Go ahead."

She sighed. The tips of her hair were singed. "The issue has been neutralized," she said wearily. "Now get your ass up here so we can figure out who sent it."

Cairo elbowed her. She only then seemed to notice Nicholas, like he hadn't been there all along. "Your Majesty," she tacked on.

6. Villain of the Piece

Nicholas waited and waited on a sound that never came.

It was the middle of the night, but he was wide awake after sleeping through most of the day. Working hard not to get his hopes up, he climbed out of bed and tested the door.

Unlocked.

The infirmary looked exactly as it had before. There was no hole in the floor, not even a scorch mark to whisper of the attack. The only difference was that Nicholas' hands had been cuffed together rather than to the bed, a precaution that might be touching if he disregarded that he was still cuffed at all, still a prisoner.

Yasmin had come by in the aftermath, her hair a good three inches shorter and a sullenness to her so severe it was like Cairo was playing his illusion tricks, casting her appearance in a smoggy cloud. But there had been no cloud as she provided Nicholas his lunch, just an unsettling lack of sunlight. It made him realize how bright she'd been to begin with, in her own turbulent, maleficent way.

Nicholas had fallen back asleep and woken up to Cairo bringing his dinner and a typical slew of nonsense. He had anticipated the click of the lock like some sad Pavlovian reject, waiting on the respite from the feeling of being watched so long that his soup was cold by the time he sipped it. And he sipped it quietly, still listening, but no click came minutes or hours later.

It could have been a stroke of good luck, but as he crept into the hallway it seemed more like a trap, the kind only the most foolish animal would fall for. What could he possibly gain from sneaking blindly around a hostile castle, except maybe a life sentence?

He continued anyway, following a nameless instinct around corners and up stairs.

He wanted his journal.

Wanted what with it, he couldn't say. Wanted to grab it and run away with it, sure, but that was a pipe dream. He might try it anyway, if he got tired and delirious enough. What more did he have to lose?

Nice try. You're not that brave.

If he was lucky, he could steal it from wherever it was locked up and stash it somewhere in the infirmary to make away with once he'd earned his freedom or figured out an escape. He could study its pages between meals until he learned its secrets. But he would have to bank on its absence going unnoticed, and he wasn't sure about those odds. He could settle just for holding it awhile.

The answers he needed might reveal themselves to him between the pages. The journal might suck him back up and spit him out in his apartment if he stared at it hard enough. He had to at least try.

He tucked himself against the wall like it might give him cover in the vast arching walkways. The torches here were like the city street lights but smaller, bulbs of fire that bounced around in their spherical glass containers, mounted on sconces. The shadows between them were just big enough to step into.

He hadn't seen guards prowling the halls when he walked them with Yasmin and Cairo and could only hope this was true of the rest of the castle. He ventured in the opposite direction of the entrance, where they were most likely to be posted, and left the rest to his crossed fingers, ducking behind columns at the slightest sound.

What was he doing?

He didn't know, but he couldn't stop. It was like he could feel it beckoning to him, his journal. Every time he approached a turn, there was a tug in his gut and he followed it. It was very possible that he was moving aimlessly, each footfall one step closer to his discovery. But he didn't think so.

He studied the walls with a skimming hand, feeling the gaps between stone slabs. A woven map of Caldora tempted him to stop and look, but he settled for slowing his steps enough to confirm that it matched his memory of his drawing, if a bit nicer. He sped up as he passed a series of paintings, overwhelmed by the history of it - royal family after royal family, chronicles of a time that didn't exist. He only lingered over the most recent portrait, a dispassionate little prince sandwiched between a lanky man and woman with his same hard chromium eyes.

What was his childhood like? Nicholas thought. Is it all fake? Does it matter if he remembers it like it's real?

The questions were endless. They hurt his head. He pushed onward, around a turn that just felt right, and he knew.

That room at the end of the hall.

His bound hands twisted awkwardly at the knob and the door crawled open on unfortunately whiny hinges. In the spirit of every welcome he'd received in Caldora so far, he was greeted by an arsenal of knives hanging in the air before him in a loose circle.

"Um," Nicholas whimpered.

They weren't knives, actually, but it wouldn't matter if they came at him fast enough. Pointed at his neck were two pairs of scissors, several fountain pens, a geometric compass, and at least twenty push pins.

The door closed loudly behind him. Not that it made much difference considering the worst person he could have run into sat on the camelback sofa, nestled into the alcove in the far wall, his face half-hidden by Nicholas' journal.

"Sleepwalking?" said Rayan.

"Yup. Yes." Nicholas let his head loll, for emphasis, and reached behind him for the door. "'M gonna sleepwalk back, now..."

The scissors lurched alarmingly close to his jugular and he flattened his arms at his sides.

In a loud theatrical whisper, the king ordered, "Wake up."

He wasn't in pajamas like Nicholas had seen him last, but his appearance was just as strange. A halfhearted attempt at proper presentation. He wore black, but his shirt was loose and billowy, wrinkled where it had been incompletely tucked into his pants and buttoned low enough to betray that he wore nothing else underneath. His hair was only halfway pulled up, and hastily so, like he had gotten tired of it falling into his eyes as he read.

He wasn't wearing his gloves. They lay in a small pile by his hip, topped with four chunky rings. Forcate flickered blue on his index finger.

"Wide awake, Your Majesty."

The deadbolt behind Nicholas clicked. There was a poetic lesson in consequences there.

"You aren't where you're supposed to be."

And regretting it more by the second. "Apologies. Your majesty."

"How did you get out of the infirmary?"

"The door wasn't locked."

"...The door wasn't locked."

"Your Majesty."

"So you came here."

They were in something of an office space, if Nicholas could reconcile a place so beautiful with the three-dimensional manila envelope that was the office he knew. It was crowded by several shelves and a broad desk, all of it mahogany, all of it laden with books. It was hard to pinpoint what exactly was so beautiful about it. The room lacked art or decoration save for a rug made of a hundred patterned squares. But there were designs carved into the doorknob and the desk had cabriole legs, and the leaded window behind the sofa didn't even have curtains, as if to say, why would you ever want to keep the light out?

"I was looking for my book...Your Maj-"

"Stop that."

"With pleasure."

His journal floated a little lower now (as did the scissors and pushpins, thankfully). Beneath it hovered a candle lined with thick waxy veins, sweating. A fat globule dripped down toward the floor and into a silver chamberstick with a gentle plink.

"How did you know it would be here?"

"I didn't. I've been looking around."

"You searched the entire bottom floor, then?"

"There was some, ah, gut feeling involved. Artistry and all that."

"Care to explain why you were roaming my halls in the dead of night in search of your confiscated diary?"

Nicholas didn't even have to lie here, not fully. "I missed it, is all."

"Artistry."

"You get it. I spent a lot of time on that thing."

Rayan leaned slowly into the cushion, hooking one ankle over the other. He was only wearing socks. It made Nicholas feel like he had walked in on something private. Rayan's body, he was beginning to understand, was much more forthcoming than his face. It was a detail that felt important. It couldn't have been less so. He was locked in an office, locked in another world, he didn't have any business thinking about his story unless he'd come up with a plan to get out of it. But he wanted badly to remember this. With the journal feet away and an assortment of pens close enough to grab (if they didn't pierce his throat first), the impulse to add a note to his first sketch of Rayan made his fingers itch. A bullet point beneath the "hard to read" already scribbled there: But not impossible. It's in his body language.

Now, that body language spoke of careful consideration, thinking. Over-thinking, but that didn't seem like something Rayan did.

Rayan slipped on his right glove. He directed the journal onto the seat next to him and gingerly caught the candle in the chamberstick, sending it to the windowsill. Everything else, he let clatter to the floor when he removed his ring. Once he had put on his other glove and his stones, he beckoned to Nicholas with two fingers. "Alright. Come."

Do I have to?

Picking carefully over the pushpins, Nicholas approached.

"You may sit."

Nicholas knelt before the couch with his hands in his lap, feeling an awful lot like a toddler at storytime. It wasn't nearly as fun as he remembered.

"You look like a toddler," said Rayan. "Do you expect to look from there, or am I to read aloud and turn the pages around so you can see the pretty pictures?"

Ignoring the honeyed condescension in his words and suppressing the hot spike of irritation that came with it, Nicholas moved to the sofa, pressed so tightly to one arm that he would've tipped over it if the wall didn't bracket him in. Rayan looked unimpressed.

He raised the book again, this time floating it somewhere between them. It opened to a scene near the middle of the story, one of Nicholas' favorites to look at. It took up both pages and had been a pain to draw; the perspective was tricky, what with Rayan leaning out of a high window of his castle on one page and Adrian surging up from the ground to meet him on the other, and both of them needing to somehow be the focus of the scene.

"I think this is the most favorably you've drawn me in the entire story."

The Rayan in the drawing had both arms thrown outward and upward and furious concentration carved around his shout. It wasn't a gracing portrayal at all.

"Emulating our sacred beast with fire." He leaned forward, tracing his finger over the flaming outline of outspread wings. "I never would have thought of that. I'm not certain I'm capable, but it is flattering."

"Is that...?" Nicholas trailed. It was hard to tell. The birdlike form was a blur of flame, but he thought the short, pointed beak spitting warning fire was familiar.

"What attacked yesterday. I wasn't sure you'd seen," Rayan said. Nicholas recalled burnt umber feathers and a fierce caw. "Can you imagine? First time I lay eyes on a true wild Fogus, and it's attacking my castle."

Nicholas' head spun. In the drawing, the fiery apparition was...it was just a bird, any bird. A flame that Rayan conjured up with vigalis, taking the shape of a massive falcon to ward off the almost-king seeking audience in his court. It was a badass defense strategy, not the imitation of some Caldoran totem. But he remembered the sickly sheen on Yasmin's face at lunchtime. Had she been forced to kill it?

And why would a sacred guardian attack its own king?

"Something amiss?" asked Rayan.

"Just. It's a lot, seeing it again."

"You care greatly for this book, don't you?"

"Isn't it obvious?"

That seemed to amuse him. "It is."

He flicked slowly through the pages. Nicholas soaked them in with hungry eyes. He wasn't any closer to having the journal in his hands, but it was a velvety relief just to be near it, roving over the pencil lines and occasional bursts of color.

At some point, Rayan started holding the journal himself. Nicholas shifted to see better, so he was leaning against the arm of the sofa rather than trying to become one with it. His eyes followed inevitably every time Rayan mapped out the drawings or followed the words with his fingers.

"Are you a pianist?" Nicholas asked. Rayan's hand stilled. Caught off guard. Nicholas was starting to see the fun in that particular game.

"I can play. But I wouldn't call myself a pianist, no."

He didn't turn the page. Nicholas warmed to the tips of his ears. Of all places to linger...

"You're very talented," said Rayan. "Though your style is strange."

"Oh. Thank you?"

"I haven't met the heir myself, but I imagine he looks quite like this. Perhaps not so...you made him beautiful."

The Adrian on the page was drawn in profile, pictured from the hip up in full color. Through his sleeveless shirt, his ribs were pulled taut with heaving breath, not from exertion but because a hand had reached out for his waist. His head was tilted up, snagging bark in his short coily hair and catching pools of moonlight in the dips above his cheeks, his deep skin nearly black in the dark. It only made the stars in his eyes all the more pronounced as he waited with plushy parted lips to be kissed. Malik leaned over him, long lashes casting longer shadows over his cheek. Adrian's hand on his jaw was large and stocky, leading to a thick arm encircled by golden cuffs and flexed with the beginnings of a tug, and then Nicholas was back to the sleeveless shirt.

The real kiss was on the next page. Nicholas had spent more time on this one, the build-up.

"Oh," he said again, and left it there. He had nothing else to say to that unless he was to admit, I made you beautiful, too.

It was true, if less immediately so. Adrian was made of softer lines and warmer colors. He had a bountiful smile. Right then, Rayan's most notable feature was probably the sleepless circles under his eyes, but that was him. Dark shades contrasted against strict pallor.

"I have so many questions about you," he said. The corners of his mouth were sharp. If he ever smiled, really smiled, it would probably be captivating. Or spine-chilling. Nicholas distracted himself with Rayan's hands flipping rapidly toward the end of the story. "Others certainly more important than this one, but you've insisted - rather emphatically - that you don't have the answers to those. Is it still selfish, then, to allow myself to ask: why am I the villain?"

He stopped on the penultimate drawing, where he hung limp from the stalk that impaled his chest.

"I told you, it isn't a reflection of my own-"

"And of all the lies I'm sure you've told me, that is the poorest," he said coolly. When he got only a fearful silence in response, Rayan added, "I've already assured you, I will not punish your honesty."

Nicholas chewed the inside of his cheek and mentally parsed through the character notes in his powerpoints and spreadsheets for something that might sound convincing coming from a Caldoran citizen. He stopped, biting down hard as a punishment for wasting seconds, and tried instead to envision the journal page he'd dedicated to Rayan. Those were the only words he could trust to be true.

"A king watches over his subjects. But how can you do that from so far away? I don't mean here, in your castle, I mean..." He pressed a palm over his own chest. Distant, he had written, a bullet point somewhere around Rayan's shoulder. Detached from his people. "You know?"

"I am very protective of my people."

"All of them?"

Rayan waited, the air heavy with expectation. Nicholas understood he had dug himself into a hole. Or created an opening, if he could make the jump.

"If you really put your effort into digging up some record of me, how long do you think it would take?" He didn't leave much room for an answer, but Rayan didn't have one. It's in his body language. Nicholas was getting good at this. He felt the momentum in his throat. "You could search forever. What's one more orphan from South Simona? You won't hurt me because I might be a citizen, you won't release me because I might be a spy. You can't prove it either way, and that's an oversight on your part, but I get to suffer for it.

"Maybe you fear that I'm both - then you would really have to reckon with your own behavior. You shouldn't worry. I don't have it in me. But my life has been shit, and yeah, maybe I've built up this evil likeness of you to take it all out on, but can you blame me? All I know of you is my own bitterness and the way people describe you. The cold, volatile, malevolent king makes for a perfect villain."

Nicholas couldn't remember the last time he'd said so much at once. It was all bullshit, every last word of it fake, but that was fiction, wasn't it? A stylized lie sewn with just enough truth to be believable. He hadn't ever liked the sound of his own voice, he found himself uninspiring on principle, but that had felt good. Like writing out loud. Like a tiny puncture in the stopper plugging his mind-to-mouth pipe, a pressurized gas leak. This king had a way of doing that, poking holes.

"And so the pecking viper finally bites," said Rayan, flipping to an early page covered corner-to-corner in sketches of imaginary beasts. He seemed to know the journal well; how many twilight hours had he spent here, studying it? The creature he pointed to was a two-tailed snake, drawn next to a sycamore leaf to emphasize how small it was. Its fangs were needle thin and still too big for its face. "So soft you might miss it. Lethal all the same. Well? Have I lived up to your expectations?"

Nicholas studied the flyaway hairs framing Rayan's face, the way his rumpled shirt hung too-big around his slouching shoulders, his socked feet tapping absentmindedly against the rug. The short distance between them on the sofa made Nicholas anxious, jittery, but it didn't make him afraid.

Not nearly. It was a disarming thought.

"The details are exaggerated. But every good villain is."

7. Jasmine

I t turned out, being held prisoner by evil mages wasn't all that bad. Boring, yes- Nicholas was starting to feel stir-crazy, which said a lot coming from someone as inactive as him. Normally when he had nothing to do, he could write. He preferred it that way. But recent events had made thinking of his story markedly bitter, and besides, it wasn't as if he had anywhere to put his thoughts down. He was used to turning to his laptop when inspiration dawned, or his notes app, or a document on his work computer, or a sticky note from someone else's cubicle. He was not above scribbling on a napkin. In the infirmary, his best option would be to carve words into a bandage with a scalpel. With his hands cuffed. It hardly seemed worth it.

At least he was in the infirmary. For the first few days, he had braced every time he heard the lock, sure he was about to be moved to a dungeon. Aside from some burn scars and scabs, his injuries were healed. Even his ankle had mostly stopped twinging. But the door opened to Yasmin or Cairo bringing a meal every time, and Nicholas was left to his own devices.

The bodyguard and the counselor were the only people he saw. Never any of the other castle staff, and never the king.

He spent most of his time in the bed farthest from the door. It wasn't any comfier than his own, but it was by the window. It had been the middle of the night the first time he'd approached it with the brilliant idea to climb out and make a run for it. Considering the infirmary was on the bottom floor, he had been reasonably shocked when he'd peered down at the ground outside and instead found a long, long drop into still water.

There was a strip of clifftop between the castle foundation and the plunge to Lake Charlatan more than wide enough to walk on, but Nicholas would be one strong breeze away from splattering like an egg yolk on the lake's twinkling surface.

He opened the window sometimes for fresh air. Those winds were no joke.

Still, he liked to stay by the window. The natural light made him feel a little less like he was decomposing, and the Caldoran night sky glittered unlike anything he'd ever seen in Seattle. Even the Montanna countryside never got so starry. Nicholas yearned to draw it.

The breeze was nice, too, from safely inside. All things considered, he could have been much worse off.

"Hiding? Boo," said Cairo from somewhere past the row of curtains. Nicholas could have sworn it had been daytime just a minute ago, but the sky outside was dusky purple. Imprisonment was making him concerningly good at dissociating.

"I'm here," he said, making his way back to the first bed. Cairo grimaced when he saw him. "Right, yeah, thanks."

"Do I have to say it?"

"You really don't."

"Should I say it?"

"No, it's okay, honestly."

"You look like a prolapsed-"

"Oh my god?"

"Sorry, too much. Perhaps you are overdue for a bath?"

Nicholas perked up. "Really?" He hadn't asked for one (he wasn't in much of a position to ask for things), but it had been a week. Though Cairo carried a tray of food, the state of Nicholas' skin took precedence over the growl in his stomach. He felt the way he assumed fish tanks did when their glass was taken over by biofilm, or like a ship hull covered in barnacles. That wasn't the writer in him exaggerating. It was alarming that he couldn't smell himself. Maybe all the sweat and sebum had clogged his nasal passages. He was willing to suffer another boiling if it meant he could be clean.

Cairo threw a black cloth onto Nicholas' face, then took a hopping step to the door and held it open, sweeping his arm across his front like he was ushering a valued guest. It helped that he was dressed even nicer than normal, head-to-toe sleek indigo satin, though the effect was ruined when Nicholas bumbled blindly past and he said, "Wow! Can't say I've smelled that before!"

It was hard to tell blindfolded, but the path Cairo took to the bath was different than Nicholas remembered. The song on Cairo's tongue hadn't changed, at least. He butchered the lyrics all the way there.

Nicholas stopped in place once Cairo's footsteps ceased. The cuffs around his wrists fell away and a door closed behind him. He took his cue to remove the blindfold, expecting to find Cairo looming over him. Instead, Nicholas heard his muffled voice through the door. "Farewell, my sweet prince! Duty calls. I'll be back to fetch you as soon as I've checked on things. No funny business!"

He locked Nicholas in. "Wait," Nicholas called, but Cairo's footsteps were already skipping out of earshot. Nicholas blinked dumbly at the scene before him.

Seven naked people blinked back.

This was not the same bath as last time. For starters, it was the size of a swimming pool, flat to the ground and framed by columns. Then there was the open ceiling. And, of course, the five ladies and two men watching him with mild disdain. They were possibly the prettiest people he had laid eyes on.

"Oh," said a girl with sepia skin and dripping hair. She looked Nicholas up and down. "Did you...get lost on your way here?"

A woman much older than the rest rounded one of the columns. She had sagging skin, bulging hips, and a face plastered with makeup. As the only other person in the room wearing clothes, she received Nicholas' full focus.

"Oh!" she echoed, which he was starting to take offense to. "Well the king does have acquired tastes, doesn't he."

A boy with the smallest waist Nicholas had ever seen on a guy clasped his hands beside his jaw and said dreamily, "I sure hope so."

"Come, then, let's get you cleaned up," said the older woman in a curling accent. "You must have had a long journey here."

"Really long," mumbled the same boy, and the girl next to him snickered.

"Stop that," the sepia girl chastised. She approached Nicholas, who stood with his back to the door long after the older woman beckoned him closer. "What's your name?"

It took a second to find his voice. "Nicholas."

He was staring resolutely past her, so he didn't notice her reaching until her hands touched his chest. A mortifying sound left him as he jumped away from her, except there was nowhere to go, so he ended up slamming the back of his head into the door and spooking her back several feet. It worked, in a way.

"I was just..." She tried to smile placatingly, but her eyes said that Nicholas was very strange. "Your shirt. Unless you want to bathe in it?"

She didn't sound sarcastic. Just perplexed, and haltingly supportive, as if Nicholas might genuinely be some freak who bathed in full linen.

"I can take them off myself," he squeaked.

Another girl, pale as marble and just as smooth, filled the space beside her, forcing Nicholas to turn his eyes to the ceiling. "Is this your first job?" she asked. "No- no one could be so lucky. Ah, is prudish your schtick? Men do love a virgin."

"How modest!" teased sepia.

"How demure," said marble, swaying with each syllable.

"I think there's been a misunder-"

He was cut off by two loud claps. "Do not waste my time, ladies," the woman crooned. "Get him in the bath; I have my work cut out for me."

"I don't think-"

"Hurry, okay?" said marble. She lowered her voice to a whisper. "Madam Bashar is mean when she feels impatient." She made claws with her hands, and Nicholas eyed the woman's nails. They looked like they'd hurt.

"Turn around," said sepia to her friend. "Have some decorum."

Giggling, they both gave him the minimal privacy of turning their backs. Nicholas deliberated slowly, weighing his options.

"What's that smell?" She sniffed the air. He hurried out of his clothes.

At least everyone else had lost interest and resumed bathing. A pair play-fought with their towels until the woman, Bashar, snapped at them.

If Nicholas forgot about the seven other people sharing it, the bath was pleasant. He took to a corner and immediately dunked beneath the warm water, cutting off any stray eyes. He tuned in to the feeling of tiny bubbles budding from his skin, taking with them days of grime. He focused on the pinprick tickles they left behind, on holding his breath, on anchoring his body downward even as it yearned to go weightless. The chatter from above was distorted, and he liked that.

"Saints," said sepia when he resurfaced. Marble was behind her, washing her hair with a foamy orange bar of soap. "Thought you'd somehow drowned in four feet of water." She held out a second bar. "I assume you'd prefer to do this yourself?"

Nicholas flushed at the prospect of onlookers watching him bathe, but she closed her eyes seconds later, humming gratefully as marble massaged suds into her scalp. Marble was too focused to pay him any mind.

Soon, he was the only one left in the bath. Everyone else milled about naked, robed, or toweling. A girl with coily hair approached from behind as Nicholas contemplated the best way to climb out with his dignity, startling him so bad he splashed her.

"Good grief, you're jumpy," she said, sitting at his back with her legs bracketing his shoulders. Something brushed the back of his neck and he splashed her again. "I actually wanted a second bath, thank you," she said dryly. "Relax. I'm combing your hair."

A towel patted over his head. "You, um. Don't have to."

"It will go faster if I do it. Now shh."

Something sweet drizzled onto the back of his hair, cool against his scalp, followed by graceful fingers rubbing it in, then a comb raking through his curls. It felt so nice, he quickly got over the bare body behind him.

She took her time detangling and didn't bother with small talk. When the job was done, she left wordlessly, like that had all been very normal. The marble girl came to Nicholas with a towel that he wrapped around his waist. Everybody was situated on stone benches past the columns now, holding small mirrors with one hand and powdering their faces with the other. They shuffled about helping each other, and Nicholas saw that easy contact and unrequested aid were normal to them. He couldn't imagine being that comfortable with anyone.

Bashar's wide hands on his back made his skin crawl. She draped a robe of blue silk over his shoulders and ushered him over to the benches, grumbling, "Count yourself lucky I always pack extras. Honestly, not even a warning! I'll have to redo the entire arrangement. What House are you from, anyway?"

Nicholas inelegantly tied the robe around his front and shimmied out of the towel. "Ma'am, there's been a mixup, or- I'm-"

"Tsk," she clicked her teeth, "You take too long. And it's 'madam.'" Her plum-colored dress and the feathers hemming her robe mopped the concrete as she whisked away to a far bench. She was back a moment later, holding what looked like a hundred strings of crystals. She clicked her teeth again. "Foolish boy, I have to take measurements."

She reached for the tie of his robe. Nicholas jumped away. "You've got the wrong idea."

The madam's whole chest lifted with an aggravated huff. "You are testing my patience."

"I'm sorry, madam, but-"

"If you have complaints, take them up with whoever sent you here."

"I don't think he meant to." The moment he heard the words in his own voice, Nicholas realized he had no grounds for them.

When Bashar reached for his robe again, Nicholas' knee-jerk reaction was to swat her hand away. Her expression turned hideous. "Touch me like that again, boy," she dared, malice on her tongue.

"Sorry! Sorry, I just-"

"You will be ready in fifteen minutes, or you will walk on your toes onto the dais." She threw the crystals at his chest. As she flounced away, she hissed, "You had really better hope that fits."

Everybody on the benches stared at him.

"You're selfish, you know?" said the boy with the waist. "Now we all have to deal with her mood."

"I've waited years for this night," snarled the other boy. "If you ruin it for us-"

"Who the hell hired you, anyway?" The girl who spoke said you like she hated its taste.

Another girl, who looked like she didn't want to be there any more than him, angrily said, "We're all fucked if you make us late. Unlike you, the rest of us have to go home with her."

It kept coming from all sides, their berating and their glares. Nicholas's mind resorted under their onslaught to its usual defense mechanism for situations such as these.

Ever the opossum, it shut down.

The marble girl took pity on him. "Why don't I help you with your make-up, first?" she offered, nodding toward a far bench. Nicholas followed her, compliant and unspeaking. He kept his eyes open as she poked around them with kohl even though it burned.

After a few minutes, sepia knelt on the floor beside the bench. Nicholas saw that the strings of crystals were actually supposed to be a costume, one that left very little to the imagination. He felt lightheaded. Had Rayan ordered Cairo to trap him here? If his move was to break Nicholas' spirit and make him talk, public dehumanization was a strong first step.

"It really is your first job, isn't it?" marble asked as she brushed through his lashes. "Chin up, love, you're very fortunate. You've reached the apex at record speed. The king's personal courtesan. It's the job we all dream of. Those of us who choose to be here, at least."

"You won't have to do much," said sepia. "Just pose around the throne, and if a man asks you to dance, dance. We'll be right up there with ya."

"I find it so peculiar that His Majesty allows his courtesans to be swept away by other men. Doesn't look very kingly."

"Look again, dear. It is a flex of his station." She puffed out her cheeks and her chest. Tightly-strung crystals shifted precariously over her breasts. "You may have them for a dance, but I'll have them for the night."

"The night?" Nicholas croaked.

"That's the idea," said marble. She leaned in close. "But Fatima's served at his birthday three years, and she says the king has never bedded even a single whore. He must be very discerning."

"Birthday?"

"What an honor it would be to earn his fancy," sighed sepia.

"Forget honor. Have you seen him?" marble fanned herself with her powder puff.

"What did Madam Bashar mean?" Nicholas asked softly. "About walking on my toes."

"Ah." Sepia's smile wavered. "She can't punish us where bruises or cuts might be visible. She'll slice the soles of your feet if you cross her."

Marble thumbed Nicholas' bottom lip away from his teeth and patted red over it. "Do you see?" she diverted. "Your only job is to sit up there and look pretty."

"I'm not..."

"You, my jewel, are very pretty."

That wasn't what he'd meant.

"What are your names?" he asked the only people who had shown him kindness since his world had flipped inside out.

The sepia girl answered Mariam, and the marble girl called herself Khadija.

When Nicholas did the mental math, it was in fact the twenty-third of July. And the king's birthday was an event that called for a ballroom.

It also apparently called for every noble Caldora had to offer. The massive room was well-filled, and everybody filling it looked expensive. Late into the night, the party was an afterimage of decorum; from what Nicholas could see, tucked into the shadow of one of the many archways lining the walls, the crowd was rowdy. Ties and updos were coming undone as esteemed guests romped to a dark, upbeat tune soaring from the orchestra on stage. Every hand seemed to hold a flute of champagne or a body.

The ballroom itself, with its ornate silver boiseries and the saints carved in metal into its ceiling, was so beautiful Nicholas normally would have stopped to wish he'd drawn it himself. His mind was a bit occupied, though, with the despair that hadn't left him since Madame Bashar herded them out of the bath through a backdoor that had been there the whole time, and the feeling of exposure that gnawed on his skin. He was fully dressed but felt more naked than he ever had.

Most of the colorless crystals hid against his hips under flowy ivory pants, but the fattest chain of them was visible. It sat beneath his navel, within the strip of midriff exposed between the pants and the matching sleeveless shirt that dipped low whenever he leaned too far forward. There were more crystals strung along his torso, and several set into silver cuffs around his upper arms. It wouldn't be so bad if he hadn't been filled in on how the night would proceed, with layers discarded every hour until every bead was on display.

Mariam and Khadija had frowned long and hard at the burn scars on his abdomen before tracing them in silver glitter. *It'll just make you all the more eye-catching,* they had placated, as if that made him feel better.

Servants emerged from the archway across from them to lay four large purple cushions on the steps of the dias surrounding the empty throne. A murmur went up. Nicholas was going to be sick.

The girls and boys from the House of Jasmine strode confidently onto the stage with a poached stray in tow. To distract himself from leeching eyes, Nicholas searched for Rayan in the crowd, packing a Yasmin-level glare.

He spotted the bodyguard's striking burgundy suit first, the tail of her waistcoat flowing around her legs like a beta fish's fin. As was her role, the king was close, but not too close. He stood in a corner talking to Cairo, reminiscent of an antisocial teenager at a party. He glanced up as cheering welcomed the courtesans' entry, but that was all. A glance, quickly disinterested once he recognized the reason for the noise. He returned to his champagne, raising the glass to thin-pressed lips. Nicholas noticed his left hand was devoid of rings. Nobody in the ballroom seemed to be wearing any, even though the noble class was made mostly of mages.

Cairo, on the other hand, surveyed the dais with mild curiosity. He did a double take, stopping mid-sentence as his face rippled with shock, sputtering something Nicholas couldn't hear from the stage but could tell was an expletive. Rayan followed his eyes. Cairo whipped a handkerchief from his coat pocket, raising it in front of the king's face just before Rayan choked on his sip.

The courtesans sank to their knees, two to a cushion, so Nicholas followed suit, dropping down next to Khadija. Rayan shoved Cairo's hand from where it wiped at his chin and started for the stage with his shoulders at his ears, but Cairo reeled him in and muttered something to him. Rayan straightened his posture, slowed his gait, and approached with all the grace expected of a king.

The crowd parted down the middle for him. Nicholas bowed with the others, hands clasped behind his back. He chanced a look and saw the king bending at the waist to his courtesans with his back to the crowd. He hadn't fully bowed his head. He was staring at Nicholas with burning eyes.

As soon as the other courtesans raised their heads, he shifted his gaze to his throne, and he walked past Nicholas to take it as if nothing was amiss.

Nicholas watched the way the drunken men in the crowd leered at the dais and wondered how the people around him, some clearly younger than him, could do this. They sat at the center of attention with unwavering grace, seemingly at ease despite the constant performance they were putting on, curving their spines and pointing their toes to elongate their legs, fanning their lashes with playful smiles. Poised unremarkably on his knees with his hands in his lap, Nicholas didn't know whether to admire them or fear for them. Then he remembered that he was right up there with them, under the same lecherous gazes. He fought the urge to let his shoulders curl forward. At the very least, he could fear for himself.

The first admirer approached the dais within a few minutes. He bowed deep and asked Rayan for 'the dark-skinned girl' without offering her so much as a nod. Rayan waved a dismissive hand, and the red-faced man led the girl who had combed Nicholas' hair into the crowd.

"You know the rules, Lord Rashi," Yasmin snapped from the edge of the dais before they got far. "Where we can see you."

Nicholas looked at Rayan, searching for answers he wouldn't find on the king's blank face. Seated on a tall throne two steps above, backed by a stained glass depiction of a fire-breathing bird, he was imposing as ever. Rayan was long, lithe, elegant in a threatening way. He had the same olivey tones as Yasmin and Cairo, but they were nearly lost on his pale skin. Tonight, the image of the Fogus warmed the moonlight, drawing out his complexion.

Rayan caught him staring. "You forget your place."

Nicholas turned his attention to the ballroom.

It went that way for some time. The first girl returned after three songs, and two more were led away. Khadija winked over her shoulder as she took a proffered arm. Nicholas hoped he would go unnoticed, surrounded by such beautiful people.

He was gripped by instant, clotting fear when a graying man stopped before the dais, poised in front of Khadija's cushion even though she had yet to return. He licked black-rimmed teeth and asked Nicholas about his evening.

"Fine," Nicholas clipped out, not at all sexy. He did not know these dances. He did not want to dance.

He was going to run. He could face the consequences later.

The man took his hand, and Nicholas stilled. He had never been good at running. Out of fight and flight, his body always chose freeze. He hated that about himself.

"If our king allows it," the man started to say, drawing Nicholas' knuckles toward his mouth. Instead of kissing them, he drew furthur to deeply breathe in the jasmine dabbed onto Nicholas' bangled wrist. "It would be my great pleasure-"

His hand was snatched away in a black-gloved grip. Rayan crouched beside Nicholas, holding the man's wrist.

"He isn't dancing."

The man's throat bobbed. Around Nicholas, the courtesans looked at each other. A clock chimed - the turn of an hour. The band switched to something lively that rapidly crescendoed, urging, and nobles hollered as Khadija kicked off her skirt. The rest of the House followed suit, though their confused glances persisted, sometimes chased with envy. Rayan dropped the man's wrist and took Nicholas.' Someone whistled at them from the crowd.

"Come with me." He tugged Nicholas past an exasperated Yasmin and underneath an archway. Howling followed them out, as well as the scandalized gawking of the entire House of Jasmine.

He didn't stop until they were far enough that the band hardly reached. Then he rounded on Nicholas with fury simmering in his eyes, and said, "What the hell do you think you're doing?"

8. When It Rains

R ayan was seething. Alone in an unfamiliar part of the castle, watching the king's fingers flex irritably, Nicholas was very grateful for whatever rule forbade wearing rings to large gatherings.

"I...what?" Nicholas said sluggishly. His body was still on the dais. His hand was still in that oily grip, scratching against a coarse beard as that man smelled his wrist.

Nicholas had spent his adolescent years and the entirety of his first and only relationship longing to feel desired. At the foot of the throne, with sultry kohl lining his eyes and light bouncing titillatingly off of the crystals at his hips, he had been looked at like a prize. It felt filthy. He wanted to pick at every inch of skin that had been ogled that way. To scrape it off and let it scab, turnover his cells so he could forget the feeling.

"Have you lost your hearing as well as your mind?" said Rayan. "You've grown too comfortable - must I remind you that you are a prisoner? You are to be seen by no one, and yet you are parading yourself at the center of my ball in-" His eyes flicked over Nicholas before quickly darting back up. "For Saints' sake, you're- this is-"

A frustrated sound came deep from his throat. His arm lunged forward and Nicholas flinched back, shoulders jumping to brace for a hit. Rayan reached past him to yank at the curtain behind him, ripping it from its rod in one pull. "Cover yourself!" he ordered.

Nicholas fumbled under the curtain's weight, bunching ultramarine fabric against his front. He was not particularly uncovered, aside from a slice of his midsection. With the window stripped, moonlight struck Rayan's form, sapping the undertones from his skin but making apparent the enraged flush on his face.

Nicholas draped the curtain across his shoulders and hugged it around himself, nestling into the safety of being closed in and covered. It was the same comfort he drew from the walls of his apartment, or even, on particularly baring work days - presentations, corrections, performance assessments - the walls of his cubicle.

"So that wasn't you?" said Nicholas.

"Me?" Rayan was incredulous. It showed in his stance, the way his shoulders drew back. But it showed on his face, too. Nicholas had expected the king's anger to be cold, contained in lowered tones and darkened eyes. This was bright, loud, erratic, spilling out all over the carpet.

"I didn't want to be up there. Cairo...I thought you put me there."

"I am not that kind of villain," Rayan sneered. He paused. "What does Cairo have to do with this?"

"He offered me a bath. But it was a different room than last time, and he locked the door, and the, um- courtesans. Were there." Nicholas curled his fingers into soft velvet. "I got swept up."

Rayan processed that in increments. "Cairo," he murmured, searching the window behind Nicholas like he could somehow find his counselor through it. His face slipped back into its usual repose, but his jaw ticked, and winds tossed behind his eyes. This was the rumbling thunder before a cloudburst. This was more what Nicholas had imagined.

"Why did you let them force you?" asked Rayan. "You should have said something."

"I did," said Nicholas.

"Clearly not."

"I did. I tried."

Rayan scoffed. "Did you." He didn't phrase it as a question, and wasn't that infuriating, as if Nicholas' answer didn't even matter.

"No one would listen."

"Then speak up!" A sudden outburst, a downpour. Rayan's eyes snapped from the window to Nicholas and he was overflowing again, feeling in full force. "Did you say something, or did you mutter and mumble and let yourself be interrupted with that wounded doe look on your face, trying to appear as powerless as a fawn? How long will you go on pretending you don't have a voice? You are practically bursting at the seams every single second - speak your mind before you blow and take my entire castle with you."

"God," Nicholas laughed. Rayan's brows lifted in surprise. "That must be so easy for you to say, isn't it?"

Maybe he truly had left his body on the dais. He found himself remarkably unencumbered as he raised his chin. "How easy as a king, to look down from your throne and urge me to speak when you have never been silenced a day in your life. How strange I must be, how deeply fucking repressed I am for holding my tongue, when an entire kingdom has hung on your every word since your first babble." He could hear his voice raising, bringing lightning to a rainstorm, but he wasn't there. No cork could plug his lungs from here.

"Have some perspective, Your Majesty. Try to imagine how it might feel not to have control of every single aspect of your life, then try to imagine feeling that for years on end, and then, try to imagine becoming somehow even more powerless in the blink of an eye. Imagine being thrown from your miserable existence into something worse, imagine being chained and beaten over crimes you didn't commit and magic you can't explain. Imagine, in the midst of that, getting locked into yet another situation you don't understand. I am scared. I am scared and I have been scared and you don't get to tell me how to work with my fear! If you're so damn worried about your castle, let me out of it."

Rayan looked ready to cut him down. "Back up," he said.

Nicholas did not remember stepping forward. At some point, the curtain had fallen around his ankles.

For all he had talked about feeling scared, right then, he was unafraid. Nicholas had thought forever that he was going numb, but he'd never imagined the breaking point would manifest like this: emotions in feverish bloom save for the one that had ruled so much of his life. Fear had frozen over, if only for a while. Could nerves be overworked? He didn't know. He wasn't thinking about it. He inched back as far as the pile of curtain allowed.

"You know nothing of the life I've lived," said Rayan. Nicholas nearly laughed again.

"I know enough." That should have been the end of it. It should have never started. But Nicholas took a full breath in and more words rode on the exhale, out of his control like everything else. "And, God, God, has it crossed your mind that those of us who live on the ground might actually have to consider how our actions affect the people around us? Every minute I took up in the baths was time the courtesans would have to pay for. Your life might be worth a thousand, but I just get the one. My discomfort doesn't warrant someone else's pain."

This time, Rayan was the one who barked a laugh. It bounced off the wall like a gunshot. "I am the king of a nation, you nearsighted clod. I have been the only royal blood in Caldora since I was a child. Every breath I take has consequences, it is all I think about."

"How's this for a consequence, then: I was forced onto that dais because you brought me here. If you're pissed that your esteemed guests saw your prisoner, take that up with yourself."

The king was slow to respond. Slow enough that the steam seemed to leach from his stance, and Nicholas started to come back to himself. Still no fear, though that may have had more to do with the almost childish chagrin on Rayan's face.

"That is not why I'm...aggravated."

"Guilt, then?"

Rayan didn't deny him. Nicholas breathed heavily with exertion that hardly seemed warranted. His throat scratched. He never raised his voice. He realized he was tired enough to curl up right there. The curtain looked very comfy.

"If it bothers you so much, why have courtesans at your birthday at all?"

Rayan grimaced. "Cairo likes to plan the parties," he grumbled. He was being so expressive. Nicholas felt like he should have been paying more attention. "But they are there willingly. It isn't...you're..."

He turned his face. Again, he reminded Nicholas of a teenager, this time poor with his words and frustrated about it.

"Yasmin," Rayan said. She appeared around a corner in the direction of the ballroom. The thought of her witnessing that exchange made Nicholas' cheeks burn. "Take him to the sick room."

"I am assigned to your side for the entirety of the event, sir," she said.

"You are assigned wherever I put you."

Yasmin's eye twitched. She dipped her head in a bow. "Of course."

She procured handcuffs from somewhere within the dramatic flare of her coat. She walked at Nicholas' back, steering him with a hand on his wrists. In the reflection in the window, he saw her raise her middle finger to her king.

They're friends, he realized. Close friends.

"'M losing it," he murmured.

"You must be, speaking to your king in that way."

And yet Rayan had not harmed him. He probably had every sovereign right. Yasmin was much easier to fear, but she squeezed his wrists after his apology and left it at that. Maybe they were all tired.

Back in the infirmary, she undid his cuffs and answered his questioning look with a flippant gesture toward his outfit. "Quickly," she said and turned her back. He could have kissed her, if he were so bold and if she wouldn't murder him.

His clothes were still at the bath, but he couldn't bear the thought of putting back on Madam Bashar's pants and shirt. He wished for another bath to wash off the lingering touch of salacious eyes, but it was enough for now to be rid of the garments that had promised more than he could give. He crawled into bed naked and pulled the cover up to his armpits, holding out his hands over the sheets for Yasmin to cuff with red cheeks.

She eyed the pile on the floor. "I'll bring a change of clothes in the morning." She sounded a little annoyed. If he weren't so used to her sounding like she wanted him eviscerated, Nicholas would not have indulged the possibility that this was her way of showing sympathy.

Sympathetic. Yasmin. Huh.

He ate his cold dinner and slept like the dead.

As promised, Yasmin brought Nicholas clean clothes with his first meal, but they weren't the pale linens he expected.

"I need your address," she said.

"My address?"

"In South Simona."

"I, um. Don't have one." At least she had turned his back to allow him to dress, so she couldn't see him cringe at his own slow wit.

"Either you truly are innocent, or you make a terrible spy."

Nicholas slowly did up the buttons of his gray shirt, the shirt he had worn to work the day his journal chewed him up and spat him into another world, buying himself time to clean up his response. "The city hasn't exactly been kind to me. I tend to float around."

Nice. Play the orphan card.

When his shirt was tucked into his pants - the black ones wearing thin around the ass - Yasmin refastened the cuffs and left him with his breakfast and scores of swallowed questions.

She was back before he could ponder them too deeply. Nicholas was staring down at the waters of Lake Charlatan, scraping the last crumbs from his plate, when, one by one, the dividing curtains swept aside until she was glaring at him across several beds. She held his work bag away from herself between two fingers as if a rat might crawl out of it.

"We are leaving," she said.

Blindfolded yet again, Nicholas was steered around several corners, pushed down into a seat. The ground rumbled beneath his feet. They were moving.

He didn't ask. He didn't dare to hope.

But when Yasmin removed the cloth from around his eyes, he was boxed in by the dark walls of a carriage, and the king's castle was a fading thing behind him, visible only when he leaned his head out of the window.

"I will make this very clear," said Yasmin. "This is not an absolution."

What reason did he have to hope? For all he knew, he was a bull in transit to a slaughterhouse.

"Many questions remain around your existence. You have yet to provide insight in regards to your crash-landing in North Simona, and you have abilities unexplained by any known magic. Until these questions are answered, you will remain under suspicion. Understood?"

Nicholas gave a stiff nod.

"That said..." Yasmin seemed reluctant to say the next part. "His Majesty has deemed these grounds as insufficient to warrant your detention. You will be returned to South Simona with all of your original possessions."

"Oh."

"Is that all you have to say?"

"You'll return my journal, too?"

"I did say all," Yasmin said irritably.

Nicholas rested his head back against the seat and parted his lips on a quiet sigh. He felt the balmy air on his cheeks, hot with Caldoran summer. In a couple of minutes, his mind would start spinning again, fast enough to hurt his head. But he figured, after everything, he deserved this. A short while to be relieved, and to feel accomplished for having made it out of one mess. Even if he didn't know how, even if the next would likely prove much harder to escape.

There it was, the spinning. The respite had only lasted a few seconds, but that was for the best. He needed a plan.

"I have a message from Cairo as well," said Yasmin. "He wanted to be the one to escort you, but it would appear he has fallen into disfavor with our king for the time being. Though it feels as if I am the one being punished."

"Sorry about that."

"He wants to explain: he did bring you into the public bath as some halfwitted joke, but he only intended to leave you long enough for a quick laugh. As the 'mastermind' behind the celebration, he lost track of time."

"Ah."

"In light of your housing situation, he is arranging for a room in South Simona that shall be yours through the next month. Should you choose to stay, he promises the utmost luxury. He has also left a sizable stack of malon with your belongings to fund any auxiliary needs. I believe that is his way of apologizing."

The spinning slowed, if just barely. That was one less issue to sort.

"He did also say he is very sorry," added Yasmin.

"Right."

"And." She pressed her lips together. "He asked me to say- and these are his words, not mine." She looked at Nicholas like she would order the driver to run him over if he did not believe her. He fervently nodded his understanding. "'You clean up nice.'"

She could have easily left that part out. She looked a bit green just from saying it. It dawned on him that Yasmin was brutal and irascible but perhaps honest to a fault. He had not written that on her page of the journal.

"If he was so busy with the party, why was he sent to bring my dinner?"

"I cannot abandon my king's side during public events."

"Why not someone else, then? A servant, or a guard, or..."

Yasmin narrowed her eyes, a swift and deadly shut down. Nicholas cleared his throat and looked out the window.

He inhaled long and slow through his nose, breathing in North Simona. Illogical as it felt to recognize a city he had never known, he was certain. He had traversed this road before, in the dead of night after his release from jail, but North Simona in broad daylight was unmistakable. The baselines were the same. Tudor-style homes crammed between wide city blocks, square buildings of brick and stone several stories high, fat streets with missing stones that snagged the carriage wheels. The smells: gravel dust tinged with coal smoke, the faint salt of the sea.

But everything had been superimposed, overlaid with layer after layer. The smells of fresh bread and spicy food cropped up from market stalls, then faded, then cropped up again. From open windows on high apartment floors, women knelt with easy balance to hook wet clothing onto hanging lines. Below them, men in roughspun fabric hollered at pedestrians blocking the paths of their horses as they lugged carts stacked with crates. Everyone made way but the children, too absorbed in their make believe. Except for one: tangy music floated through the carriage window as a boy blew into an odd brass instrument from the side of the thoroughfare, kicking his feet whenever passerby dropped coins into his cooking pot.

This was the center of Caldoran commerce and trade. This was a sketch on a map and a handful of words in his journal, propped up to stand on its own. It wasn't enough to say it had been brought to life. It had been brought to one-hundred-thousand lives.

In time, the buildings thinned and so did the crowd. They drove by industrial vats that stunk of tar. A stone wall stretched for what felt like a mile. "What's that building?" Nicholas asked. He opted not to look at Yasmin, in case she was trying to evaporate him with her eyes for speaking.

But she answered, "Pondtam Prison."

Pondtam. They were just outside of geographical North Simona, still within reach of its metropolis. In another storyline, Nicholas could have wound up here. He remembered the mad woman with the albino rat across from his cell at the jail. She called me a witch! And you know the fate of a woman called a witch.

"Is this where witches are executed?"

Yasmin let out a sharp breath. "Witches have not been hanged for generations. Those rumors would do well to dispel themselves."

"But they are imprisoned," Nicholas guessed. "For how long?"

"It is a serious crime."

"Creating a love potion? Or simply having the power to?"

"Love potion- what are you talking about? The kova zem they command are difficult to obtain and impossible to control except at their hands. The other gifted are at their mercy. You know the story of Delilah; you understand why another powerful witch cannot be allowed to rise. It is dangerous magic."

Actually, Nicholas hadn't understood half of what she'd said. He understood this, though: "Like mine. They're guilty for existing outside of your comprehension."

"Watch yourself. You serve a charitable king. If you are so determined to call yourself guilty, we can turn back to al-Narin this instant. Or we can drop you off right here."

It was not the time for laughter, but Nicholas found himself fighting down a smile. Al-Narin. It was written somewhere around page seven of the journal, above his drawing of the castle. Around it, several other names had been scribbled and crossed out. The name of the Caldoran castle had been a blank spot on his documents for years, a question mark on his spreadsheets. Al-Narin was more of a placeholder than a final verdict, but he supposed the decision was final, now.

He could sense the journal, tucked into his work bag, closer than it had been since that night in the study. He would have his hands on it soon. The thought made him restless all over. If he kept shifting in his seat, he was going to really wear a hole through his pants.

The drive took them inland through countryside and village, industry and excavation. When the sun set, the road was nearly black in most places, until they crossed through towns busy enough to light them. Normal torches and lamps lined the roads; few mages lived this far from al-Narin.

Nicholas felt too anxious to sleep, and yet at some point during the night, when the horses stopped to rest, he blinked and opened his eyes to a bright afternoon. He wiped the corner of his mouth with his sleeve, aware of Yasmin's disgusted side-eye, and looked out the window at South Simona.

It was much like its sister city, but stockier. The smell of the sea had returned.

"It will be a while," said Yasmin. "The hotel Cairo arranged is at the city's far edge."

At this rate, Nicholas might just forgive him. The plan was practically forming itself.

In front of an establishment that could only be described as palatial, Yasmin unlocked Nicholas' handcuffs for the last time and handed him a contract and a pen.

"The terms of your release," she said. "You'll find the main one is silence."

Nicholas signed. He was handed his bag. Inside were his laptop, his phone, his wallet, his keys, work miscellaneous, and his journal. He took it out, opened it to the first page just because he could. The ridges of the paper felt like home beneath his fingers.

"Get out," said Yasmin.

He shuffled onto the side of the road and remained there long after the carriage had shrunk to nothing, single-mindedly fixated on the page.

The Lovers. Shrouded as she was in darkness, he may not have recognized the woman in the drawing if not for the steaming pond she knelt by and the oleander bushes dotting the garden. The crumpled, broken body she reached for had danced in Nicholas' dreams. And then she had burned, and he had wilted.

The sketch didn't have anything to do with his story. It had been a warm-up, a way to flex his fingers. But this woman had appeared in his dream. He remembered it vividly even a week later. That was not normal for his dreams.

You are not supposed to be here. So we're doing the impossible now, are we? I didn't think that was allowed, anymore. Well, anyway. Welcome.

Clutched by the sensation that he was nudging at something important, he bumbled into the foyer of the sort of building he normally didn't even dare look at for too long. It was gorgeous at sunset, but he hardly noticed, head buried in his book. He only glanced up to reach the concierge, oblivious to the curled lips of the affluent patrons. Nicholas gave his name and received his key.

As promised, the accommodations were luxurious. Nicholas sank onto the most comfortable mattress his ass had ever touched and studied the journal's third page. A tray arrived for him unrequested. He filled his stomach on a steaming dish that reminded him of kabsa, flicking back and forth between his maps.

He had claimed South Simona as his home with no particular plan in mind. It was a hugely populated city, and it was close to the frontier - close to Interra. That was all he'd had to go off. You clever bastard, he congratulated himself.

The stack of malon in the front pocket of his bag was more than sizable. He couldn't say he was grateful for the night of the king's birthday, but he would absolutely capitalize on Cairo's blunder. And his deep pockets.

He returned to page three. At the pit of the grassy valley that marked the cleavage between Caldora and Interra, Halcifer School of Magic stood tall despite centuries of neglect, overtaken with weeds but just as grand as al-Narin. Even in two dimensions, it seemed to radiate ancient power. This was a castle that would not crumble.

Nicholas would take a page out of Adrian's book. The almost-king had run from his coronation fast and hard, all the way onto the frontier; there, he had sought answers from Halcifer and its deep history. Nicholas was not a hero, but he could think like one. He had written one, after all.

9. Déjà vu

The road ran out, crumbling into a dead end in a heap of upturned stones. The chaise came to a stop in a town Nicholas couldn't name, and the driver held out his hand for a tip with a disinterested curl to his lip, like, I don't know why you'd willingly come here and I don't care to.

Nicholas was having trouble remembering himself. The town was an abandoned urban plan, overtaken by foliage but hardly scenic. What buildings still stood were dilapidated. The people sitting around them, too. They looked hungry. As Nicholas rose, the weight of his work bag dragged his shoulder downward. Or maybe that was just guilt, because he had jammed it full of as much food as it could fit on Cairo's dime back in South Simona. He would need it, he knew that, but he had never been comfortable with excess.

He handed the driver a couple extra malon. His parents smiled at him from the ID slot of his wallet, the kind of smiles that scrunched their cheeks and noses and nearly closed their eyes. His father used to remind him to look to his ancestors for guidance, but Nicholas had never bought that a bunch of Brazilian spirits could help him through twenty-first century American growing pains from across the Atlantic. He wondered if he would be able to ask his father for answers now, had he tried harder to understand back then. There was much more than an ocean in the way now, though.

He can still help me, Nicholas thought. He always has.

The driver cleared his throat. Nicholas muttered an apology, half-standing in the chaise, and climbed out.

"Excuse me," he said to a man slouched against a sagging wall. "Which way is the frontier?"

Though Nicholas did not know the town, he had an idea of where he was. The last two towns before it had been much the same. Some centuries ago, long before Caldora and Interra, the land had probably been lush. But overfarming had sapped the soil, and before the land could recover, cities had cropped up where farmland once stood. Or, they had tried to, but as one kingdom split into two and the new nation of Caldora shifted inward, these towns had sunk, forgotten, to the outskirts. They fell under a common name, the Borderturf.

The man raised his jutting chin. His tongue poked heavily between his remaining teeth. "No one ever tell ya knowledge got a price?" he said, looking Nicholas up and down. Nicholas doubted this knowledge was particularly valuable, but he procured another few bills for times' sake - and to make his bag feel a little lighter. The man grinned, gummy and sly, and pointed straight down the deteriorated street. Well played.

Picking between the overturned stones, Nicholas avoided eye contact with the scarce townspeople eyeing his bag. They were all sitting outside, soaking in the sun. Or rotting in it. He opened his journal to Rayan's page. Distant. Detached from his people.

Nicholas walked for miles. The road eventually faded to nothing; the buildings grew sparse, then disappeared. The land turned bright green beneath his feet. He continued on, waiting for some landmark or sign to tell him he was crossing the border onto the frontier. It wasn't until he checked behind him and found himself nowhere that he realized he was already there.

All around him were shallow hills dotted with low trees. Clutching the compass he'd purchased the evening before, he swiveled this way and that until his body pointed south. Nicholas sat, ate an apple and a chunk of bread, and watched the clouds roll above him. They were long, thin, and slow. Stratus, he guessed. He studied his map of Caldora, but there wasn't much it could do for him now. There was South Simona, then the Borderturf south of it, then the frontier: a wide channel of land that hadn't been lived on for centuries. Nicholas could make out the remains of a countryside. Scattered gravel, mounds of mossy stone that might have once been walls - this was all that remained of the Kingdom of Maesia.

It looked the same in every direction. Nicholas could only rely on his compass and his intuition.

His dad had always been unrelentingly clever. It used to frustrate Nicholas to no end, how Bruno would find the best hiding places and Nicholas would have to either search for hours, or let go of his young pride to accept an assist; how the classroom letters Nicholas wrote to his mom would never measure up to Bruno's love poems. He tried to channel his dad's shrewdness now, surrounded for miles by lonely land.

He did not rest long. He didn't want to find out how a magicless twenty-something would fare in these open fields after dark.

For hours he walked due south beneath the unforgiving sun. He stripped to his undershirt and tied the button-up around his waist to feel less like he was melting, with the trade-off of feeling like he was burning instead. He did not burn easily, but Caldoran July was no joke.

When he thought he wouldn't make it any further, the dips of a valley came into view. In a misguided surge of triumph, Nicholas kicked into a run.

He regretted it immensely as he slumped down in a clump of shrubs, hacking for breath, trickling water from his canteen from several inches above his mouth for fear that he would suck it dry if he got his lips on it. His ankle hurt for the first time in days. He had forgotten himself for a second there. He'd almost believed he could be the kind of whimsical, tireless character he so loved to write about. But that was fiction for a reason. Nicholas was unathletic and difficult to excite, and when he tried to rise to someone else's energy level, he fell. That was how it had been for as long as he could remember.

He pushed onto wobbling legs and started east on an inflated hunch. He didn't have any real way of knowing where he was in relation to Halcifer, but he did have a loose idea of his position relative to the ocean, a drawing of the valley, and enough desperation to drive him onward. He tried to match the shape of the river at the base of the valley to the line snaking through his sketch and felt like a delusional fool.

"Starvation. Dehydration," Nicholas muttered beneath his breath as he pushed forward on aching feet. The sun was beginning to dip alarmingly low. "Predation. Territorial magic beast attack. Pecking viper bite." He tripped over a rock. "Several-hundred-foot-tumble-"

Something with teeth clamped down around his left foot and pulled, because one bad ankle wasn't enough. He went feet-first over the ridge thrashing and yelling. In a tragic but typical turn of events, he fumbled for his new pocketknife, cracked his knuckles painfully against a rock, and lost his grip as his fingers went numb. Nicholas didn't know what was pulling him. He didn't keep his eyes open long enough to find out. Thanks to the river, the valley walls were lusher than the land above, so he had plenty of trees to crash against as he was dragged down the slope. Clutching his bag to his chest with one arm and guarding his head with another, he gave in to his fate and hoped he had taken after his mom's tough skin, too.

When the dragging stopped, he lay prone in the fetal position with his eyes squeezed shut, and asked whatever saints watched over this land, "Why?"

He managed to pry his eyes open in spite of the layer of dirt caking his lashes together. He checked his bag before he checked himself for injuries, a real modern day materialista.

His laptop was in two separate pieces. He couldn't tell the back of his phone from the front.

"Why," he groaned again, mournful.

Every muscle and bone creaked in protest as he shouldered onto his forearms, but nothing seemed serious. At least, nothing other than the plate-sized venus flytrap secreting enough liquid onto his leg to soak through his sock. His ankle itched.

It wasn't done yet. Its stem recoiled inch by inch, slowly drawing Nicholas another few feet through the brush.

"Hey...hey!" A voice shouted through the trees. "I think she caught something!"

"Oh no," Nicholas mumbled. He pried at the plant's mouth, but it held fast. "Oh no, no, no."

He pounded his busted phone against one of its green lobes until his fist crunched through the cellulose. The plant went limp. He scrabbled to run for it, hands slipping in the dirt.

"Oh...shit," the same voice said, this time much closer. Nicholas looked over his shoulder and stilled, hunched on his hands and knees.

The young man gawking at him stood in a perfect ray of light, as if the trees themselves had parted for him. It made his deep brown skin glow, but maybe that was just him. He had a handsome face that Nicholas knew almost as well as his own, a perfectly proportioned alloy of Filipino and afro-latino features - like Nicholas, if Nicholas was gorgeous. It was a face befitting a king.

Adrian was no king, though.

"Aw, I can't eat you," he lamented. "And you killed my plant! I spent a whole day growing her."

"Guh," Nicholas said to the hero of his story.

Adrian's pout melted into something sheepish. "Oh." He ran one hand over close-cropped hair. A borrowed tunic strained across his broad chest, cut at the sleeves and below the waist to reveal the jewel dangling from his navel and the four golden cuffs on his arms. One around each forearm, one around each bicep, all inlaid with precious stones. It was a wonder they didn't snap when his arm flexed. "Are you alright, though?"

His gentle accent was different from the one Nicholas had grown used to in Caldora. A little curlier, more romantic. It reminded him of Bruno.

"Shit," Adrian said when Nicholas continued to gape at him. "You must have hit your head."

"Uh," said Nicholas. "Nah."

"Must've hit it bad."

Adrain cupped his hands under Nicholas' armpits and lifted him easily to wrap an arm around his waist. Nicholas, still suffering from his fall and probably diagnosable shock, let himself be hauled like lumber along the path carved out by the stem of the venus mantrap.

They came upon a simple house of log and stone. Distantly, Nicholas could hear the river. It would have been an unassuming home if not for the garden that fanned outward from its front wall like something out of Wonderland, growing taller than the building itself. Broad leaves cast umbrella shadows, carrot heads poked like groundhogs from the dirt, and Nicholas couldn't even see the tops of the sunflowers. At the center of it, a leggy man sat on a rocking chair in a patch of sun, hand outstretched to stroke absentmindedly over a rose thorn as big as a knife.

"I thought you were going to catch me a meal," he said.

"Well I didn't exactly anticipate a person taking an evening stroll through uninhabited land."

"We're habitating it."

"Yeah, so, that isn't really what I'm getting at here?"

"And did you, pray tell, ask this person why he might be passing through no man's land near dark?"

"I think he's concussed."

"Have you forgotten what side of the river we're on?"

Nicholas was unceremoniously dropped to the grass. Thick vines crawled out of the dirt to loop around his ankles.

"You've gotten quick with that."

Adrian looked pleased. "Haven't I?"

"Focus."

"Right." Adrian tried to loop another vine around Nicholas' neck, but the instant it touched his skin, its growth ceased. "Uh, Malik? I think he's Interran. And powerful."

Nicholas finally spoke up. "I am neither of those things."

"Hey, don't sell yourself short." Adrian gave him a sympathetic nudge with his foot. Then his eyes hardened. "You are Caldoran, then?"

"Nope, no, just incredibly lost."

Adrian scrunched up his face. "See what I mean? Concussed. I'm going to lay him down inside."

Malik said, "Do not just-"

"He is hurt. And it's my fault. I am taking him inside."

They stared each other down. For someone who had run away from his throne, Adrian sure held his head like a king. The look in his eyes invited a challenge, but in the same breath warned that it would be swiftly trampled. It was just as Nicholas had imagined, and even more potent off the page. Malik eased back into his seat, conceding.

"Do not forget whose house this is," he said as Adrian freed Nicholas and helped him inside.

"You remind me every day," sneered Adrian.

The house's interior was hot and snug. The largest window was lined with flower pots, and though the plants within were normal-sized, their assortment was just as unusual. Nicholas recoiled as a venus flytrap closed its maw around an errant fruit fly. The furnishings carried the air of some-thing crafted by hand, a spectrum of mismatched shades of wood and carving styles that traversed half a century. Here were three generations of homemade effects, each reflecting the maker's style.

"Easy does it," murmured Adrian as he lowered Nicholas onto a yellow sofa with fraying edges. Instead of standing, he knelt at Nicholas' eye level and lowered his voice conspiratorially. "You can tell me, now. I know Malik seems frightening, but he has yet to harm me. Aside from when he tried to stab me in my sleep, but that was a whole week ago- water under the bridge, really. I think...he is probably kind. He is..." Adrian pouted, considering. "He is Caldoran, but he isn't like his people. He does not wish to be. That is why he's here."

Nicholas, of course, knew all of this. He knew that Malik was not nearly as uncaring as he liked to portray, that he had simply been lonely for so long he'd forgotten how to be around people. In many ways, he'd never learned. More than once, Cici had written next to his dialogue, *Estás proyectando*. Which, rude.

"But why are you here?" asked Adrian. "From which part of Interra do you hail? How did you come to wield crescia and vidia that way, too? I only just learned it was possible myself, and I-"

"You made that trap," Nicholas realized. He pressed the heels of his palms to his eyes. His head had started pounding, and it had nothing to do with the summer sun or his slide down the valley wall.

"Does it hurt? Do you need anything? I'm hopeless at this. I'll be right back."

Nicholas was in the same position when he returned minutes later. "Some water, and berries if you're hungry," Adrian said. "You really don't know who I am, do you? Saints, how hard did you hit your head?"

"I know you very well," said Nicholas.

"Oh. People normally bow, you know?" Adrian gave a halfhearted laugh. "You haven't asked. About my coronation. Surely the entire kingdom must've heard by now. Unless...how long have you been out here?"

"I know that, too. I know everything about that."

"Hold on, you should-"

But Nicholas was already pushing himself upright. He heaved a tremulous breath. "I know so much."

"Alright, you're starting to scare me."

"I'm a writer. Fiction."

"Er, cheers?"

"I wrote a story. About a prince who hid away in the forest to run from his coronation, and didn't stop running until he stumbled across a house on the frontier where a man from his rival kingdom lived alone."

Adrian squinted. "Oddly familiar."

"Where I came from, it was a fantasy. Every last second of it was utterly impossible. I named my hero Adrian and wrote this- this journey where he finds himself and falls in love and learns what it means to be a king, and- and-"

Nicholas had started slowly, but his tongue was running away from him now. Relief hammered his chest open; his lungs swelled to fill the space. Because Adrian was good, and brave, and warm, and finally, Nicholas could talk about this. He could come clean and stop driving himself insane. He could ask for help.

"I put it in a journal." He grabbed the book, shaking it. "This journal. And then there was this- sucking feeling, into the journal, then I was hurtling through I don't even know what, and then it spat me out in the capital of Caldora and I have had, just, a historically terrible time ever since. And this whole time I just assumed I had somehow been sucked into the world I created, but now you're here, exactly where you should be, so I'm- I'm in the middle of the story itself. I'm talking fully fucking submerged in the plot, like, post-inciting-incident but pre-rising-action-"

"Oh, so you're fully mad," said Adrian. "Or severely concussed."

"No!" Nicholas heard the frantic cry in his own voice and took a deep breath. Pick your words carefully, don't say too much. Talk for too long and they'll stop listening. He was breaking all of his own rules. "No. I know it sounds crazy. But I'm from this place called Earth where there's no magic, no Interra or Caldora. I don't know how, but this book brought me here. Look."

He opened to an early page. Adrian's face drew inward angrily. "Have you been stalking me?"

Malik entered. He paused in the doorway, looking between Adrian's scowl and Nicholas' too-bright eyes with one raised eyebrow. He continued past them to the kitchen.

And paused again. Malik turned around and, with a subtle beckon, yanked Nicholas' bag toward himself. The pull forced Nicholas off the sofa in a squawking heap, and would have towed him across the floor had the strap not come loose from his shoulder. Malik caught the bag with one hand and ripped something from its front.

"You should be more selective with your friendship," he said to Adrian, turning something over in his palm. He held up a small shiny rectangle, one of the buckles that held the bag closed. "I have half a mind to cut you open for letting a mole into my home."

Oh, Nicholas thought, you can't be serious.

10. Square Peg, Round Hole

The Faisan family line went further back than Caldora itself. During the bloody division of Maesia, among the first and strongest soldiers to fight for Caldoran magic were a man and a woman with only three stones between them - inercium and forcate on her side, encaline on his. No matter who married into their bloodline across the generations to come, no other stones were ever mastered by their children. It was dubbed "the curse of the Faisans," though curse was something of a misnomer. Their lineage moved mountains.

Caldoran code demanded that all mages in control of at least four stones served the kingdom. In the fine print, an exception: if called upon, specified three-stone wielders could also be levied. No names appeared anywhere in the law, but it was universally and tacitly known that this stipulation had been devised to keep one particular family tethered.

It worked for hundreds of years, until the lineage bore a tameless spirit who scorned her predetermined life of obligation. She faked her family's death in a mansion sent up in flames and fled to the frontier with her husband, her son, and her daughter in law, and so ended the Faisan name.

That woman was Malik Faisan's grandmother.

The last direct notch in a legendary family line, Malik passed his days tending to his garden and rereading the archive of books left behind for him. They were factual but entertaining, mostly chronicles by Faisans who had witnessed the history firsthand. It was a peaceful life, if not the most exciting for a young man in his prime.

Or, it had been, until a stranger crash-landed in his gardenias.

Their cloak was filthy. That was all Malik had time to note before the Mingles descended.

They flocked the stranger with talons and fangs, batlike wings swarming into a stormcloud over Malik's garden. The stranger's hands lashed out from beneath the cloak. Malik knew at once he was Interran - he'd be stupid not to. The bands around his arms were not subtle. Neither was the jewlery dangling from his ears when his hood fell away in the struggle. Not just any Interran, then. Noble birth. A strong fighter, probably, but the river was too far to do him any good, and the rocks he flung skyward with the mossy gem on his wrist were too slow for the nimble brutes.

Malik did not step outside to help him. He had learned wariness before he learned kindness; if somebody was to appear on his doorstep, he was to bury their body. This was the only way to protect his freedom. The Mingles would make his life easier.

Huge black eyes caught Malik's through the window. The stranger must have seen on Malik's face that he planned to watch him die, because he did not bother pleading. He narrowed his eyes, accusing, determined, and sprung back into his hapless fight.

Malik felt himself freeze from the inside. Then he felt himself run through the door.

When the battle was over, and the Mingles hung limp from stone stakes jutting from the flowerbed - his poor masterworts - the Interran said, How did you do that? He was looking at Malik's rings. At least he was not stupid, either.

Malik dressed Adrian's cuts with salve he made himself and fed him from the garden. When Adrian asked for a bed to lie in, Malik gave him the second room. And that night, when regret and hard-taught fear got the better of him, he knelt at Adrian's bedside with a knife pointed at his chest.

Adrain caught his wrist mid-strike and fixed him with that same narrowed look. He did not move to leave the next day, and Malik did not make him, though his stilted hospitality came at a price. In exchange for a room in his home and food off his table, he demanded labor.

If you knew who I was, Adrian bristled. He disliked like this man and his tone. He was not a servant to be driven.

Are you going to tell me? asked Malik, to which there was no response. It matters not. Whoever you think you are, whoever you might have once been, to me you are nobody. I am the king of this land. A man who runs from his title has no right to wield it as a weapon.

They weren't friends. It was a delicate peace, only one week old and yet to open its eyes. Nicholas was a sledgehammer.

"Eavesdropper," Malik said. When he closed his fist around the buckle, the black encaline on his little finger glowed yellow. "It would take a skilled mage to place such a robust charm on so unassuming an item. Somebody high up the Caldoran food chain has been listening to your every word."

Adrian grayed. Nicholas clambered onto his knees.

"I had no idea," he swore. "It was probably the king-"

"The king?" Malik and Adrian said at once.

"I am going to leave your body for the birds," said Adrian, leering over him.

"Not inside," said Malik.

"Let me explain," pleaded Nicholas.

The stones cuffed around Adrian's arms began to glow. "You have thirty seconds."

It was the best thing he could have said. It calmed Nicholas down. He had spent his life packaging his thoughts into digestible pill capsules. With practiced, almost instinctual ease, he reigned them in with a ball and chain and forced them into bite-sized pieces.

That didn't make them easy to swallow. "Do you honestly expect us to believe our lives began a week ago?" said Malik.

"Or that Rayan would let you go out of- what, the kindness of his heart?" scoffed Adrian.

"I have twenty-three years of memories that beg to differ."

"That man's idea of mercy is a speedy execution."

"Care to explain my collection of history books?"

"He would mount your head on his wall."

"Magic doesn't work on me." That gave them pause. "You saw earlier. The vines. For some reason, your magic just- nullifies when it touches my skin."

Without warning, Malik sent the buckle flying for the space between Nicholas' eyes. He barely got his hands up in time. The impact stung a little, but the buckle dropped instantly. The stones on Adrian's upper arms, one orange and one yellow, flickered as a stringy plant on the windowsill wound toward Nicholas, elongating rapidly from the stalk. When it was right in front of his face, Nicholas poked the black flower at its tip, and the growth stopped.

"Ta-da?"

"I don't see any zem," Malik said dubiously.

"Should we make him strip?"

"I'd rather not."

Nicholas lifted the bottom of his shirt.

"Are you deaf as well as mad?"

"Something burned me when I crossed over," he said. "I still don't know what. But your gemstones- uh, zem? They burn when I touch them, too."

"Kova zem," said Adrian. "Blessed stones. You really don't know?"

"Do not play into his tricks," hissed Malik.

"My story. It's accurate, isn't it?" Nicholas held up his journal, but Adrian quickly snatched it away.

"We've already established that you're a stalker."

"There's more, stuff that hasn't even happened. A stalker can't tell the future."

"No," Adrian said darkly, curling his fists, "but perhaps a witch can."

"Nobody can," said Malik. "There is no foresight, even in the most powerful witchcraft."

"I don't even know what witchcraft is," Nicholas maybe whined, a little. "How about this: you two hold onto the book, hide it if you want to. It's more important to me than anything right now, so you have leverage, or whatever. If something happens that's written in there, you'll know I'm telling the truth."

"How about this?" echoed Malik. Another object flew at Nicholas' forehead. Adrian caught the kitchen knife by the hilt before it could lobotomize him, arm taut against the pull until Malik released his magic with an aggreived sigh. "You can't seriously believe him."

"I don't! I don't. But you can't just kill him."

"You've grown comfortable," Malik growled. "You will not give me orders in my home."

"I will when you behave like an unsocialized animal."

The ebony side table slammed into Adrian's chest. He careened back into the wall, coughing for breath, bracketed between its fluted legs. Just as quickly, the stringy plant surged in size. Soil showered the rugs as it burst from its pot, fat tendrils winding around Malik's ankles, wrists, and the braid hanging down his back.

"Don't you dare," said Malik. The plant forced his chin high. "I gave you that power."

Nicholas, who was still seeing the residual frames of his life flashing before his eyes (it was a pretty depressing montage), watched this all unfold from the floor.

"You didn't give me jack. You opened my eyes, and I am trying to return the favor. Regardless of how many lies he's told, if there is any possibility that my future lies in his book-"

"Then we'll kill the boy and keep the book."

"I will watch him," said Adrian. "Day and night. "If it comes to it, I will kill him. You have my word."

"What good will your word do me?"

"I swear on my country."

They looked at each other for a long time.

"I'm taking the book," said Malik.

Adrian's cheeks puffed like he was physically holding back an argument. "Just. You shouldn't look at it. It may influence your actions. We won't know if it truly predicted anything."

"Fine," Malik spat. He beckoned, and the journal soared into his hand from the floor. The plant unraveled. The table drifted back into place.

"Share the room. Do not let him out of your sight." Malik swept toward the kitchen, taking the journal and Nicholas' bag with him. "And you- change, you're filthy. If you cut my clothes, I will cut off your hand."

He glared at the frayed hemlines of Adrian's ensemble. Adrian smirked, tugging at the ends of linen shorts that had very clearly once been pants. "It isn't my fault you're as thick as a prairie cat."

Malik slammed the door. Adrian sagged against the wall, and in the waning daylight, Nicholas noticed the way his cheeks seemed to sag, too. He looked exhausted.

"Reckon it's too early for bed?" he asked.

The sun had only halfway set. "Not at all."

Nicholas should have considered before agreeing that bed really meant bed. As in, bed, singular.

"Don't be an old maid," Adrian taunted. "It's spacious."

Nicholas changed into clothes that hung past his heels and wrists. Adrian did not do him the decency of turning away. Nicholas heard him shuffle closer and yelped, hurriedly pulling the pants over his ass.

"What's this?"

Nicholas spun. Adrian was sliding what was left of his phone from the pocket of his discarded pants. No amount of dry cleaning would fix those grass stains.

"Proof," said Nicholas. "Technology from Earth."

"It looks like a chunk of metal and shattered glass."

There was no fixing that, either. If only he could trade in Cairo's cash for USD when he got home. If he got home. "Yeah, it does now."

"Tell me your name."

"Nicholas."

"I swore on my country, Nicholas. You understand the weight of that."

"Yes. Your Majesty."

"So do not give me a reason to kill you."

"I won't."

Adrian sat heavily on the side of the bed closest to the window. "I didn't quite make it to 'Majesty.' I'm not anybody, anymore. What I mean to say ...Adrian is fine. In front of the Caldoran, you don't know me as anything else. Is that clear?"

"Super."

"Do you plan to sleep standing? That might make me distrust you more than anything."

Nicholas perched on the very edge of the bed. Adrian chuckled. "What, never slept with a prince before? Joking! Don't look so sickly, you'll offend me." He laid a pillow down to bisect the bed. "There. Strict sides. No crossover."

Nicholas sat against the headboard stiff as a log while Adrian crossed his arms behind his head and stretched out his legs, looking every bit like he'd been spun from golden thread as the sunset shifted over his skin. It clung to the high points of his cheeks, trickled into the dips along his arms, his legs, his midriff, then gradually gave way to shadow. Somehow the lines of him were even more pronounced in the dark. Nicholas looked away.

"I will not believe that every choice in my life was made for me. Would you?"

Nicholas admitted, "I might." He wouldn't mind having someone to blame.

"I shudder to think you know everything inside my head."

"Not everything."

Adrian shifted onto his side. "What must I do to coax more than three words out of you?"

"Invasive brain surgery, probably," mumbled Nicholas.

"Four! And they were funny." Adrian rested his cheek in his palm. He had the kind of smile that made Nicholas feel red in the face. "I'll confess, it's a worthy shame that you are almost definitely out of your mind. Or a stalker."

Nicholas turned his back, tucking himself up to his cheeks. "Goodnight."

"Sleep beautifully, Nicholas."

He didn't sleep much at all, no matter how ruefully his body called for rest. He kept waiting for Malik to appear at his bedside with a knife, or for Adrian to roll over the pillow between them and choke him. Rest came in short sprints. He only knew he'd been drifting off when the paranoia won out and he checked over his shoulder, and Adrian's strict side was empty.

□ □ □

On Adrian's first day in the Faisan home, he was told to tend the garden. It was careful work. With the crescia stone on his right arm, he urged seeds to germinate and unraveled flower buds into full-bloom. Too much, and they would wilt.

On his third day, Malik asked him to grow a tomato the size of a pumpkin.

That's not possible, said Adrian.

A small pumpkin.

That's not possible.

Crescia, the growth stone, did not defy nature. It sped up natural process-es, but it couldn't reshape them. Interran magic seldom sought to alter a target at its essence; such work was perverted, sacrilegious. It was the work of Caldoran mages. It was the death of Maesia.

There was one exception, a power that could splice together shredded skin and seal fractured bones. Such a talent, the gift of healing, would never be scorned by a people who so celebrated life. But of the nine minerals wielded between the two kingdoms, a baby born with vidia was the rarest. And even among those blessed few, it was not a stone easily controlled.

How are you so certain? said Malik. He knelt, pressing a palm to the grass, and three stone spires coiled out of the ground, sloughing dirt from their tips. Is it also impossible for a Caldoran to command the earth?

It should be. Yet here you are, again.

A smile, the first one. Here I am.

If vidia was the power to rewrite, and crescia was the power to grow, then together they were reconstruction.

But Adrian was stubborn. It doesn't work like that.

Have you tried?

It's...unnatural.

Right, right. To your people, distortion defies the land. Mine would say the same about tapping into it for your own advantage. They were the same people once, don't forget, with the same gifts. Until they became so entrenched in their principles that they willingly gave up their own power, and now it's been too long and that power is lost, and isn't that a shame. What was taken for granted cannot be regained. But we are not as limited as we think.

The secret to the Faisan family strength was this: long after the dust had settled over the chasm between their nations, they still thought like Interrans.

What is the difference between a stone inlaid in a wall - Malik stroked the house's foundation and pulled from it a small stone arrowhead - and one buried beneath the soil?

The latter is connected to the land. Your magic cannot touch it.

Cannot, cannot, cannot, Malik mused as he touched the ground again. Stop leaning over me, he said, seconds before an identical arrowhead shot from the ground and through the air, into the belly of a sparrow passing overhead. It is all unnatural. Hungry?

□ □ □

Nicholas heard footsteps through the wall, soft and lightweight. Malik. It was still dark outside. The front door opened and closed, and Nicholas crept into the main room. He would be the only one there for some time. This was routine.

Malik's voice hummed through the wall, "...not to let him out of your sight."

"He is sleeping," said Adrian. "And seemingly rather weak."

"I read the book."

This was not routine. These early hours between them were supposed to pass quietly.

There was a slam that rattled the door. Nicholas flinched away. "What is wrong with you?"

"Calm yourself, bull brain, I lied," Malik said, slightly choked. "Still clueless as a lamb, just as you like me."

"I tire of your games."

"I don't like that the two of you know something I don't."

"You hardly know anything at all, hermit."

"Who is the man you are so desperate to bury."

"What does it matter to you? You told me he was nobody, and then you put him to work. So let me work."

"You blundered onto my land hardly able to stand on your own two feet and tried, from your knees, to command me. Do you know who behaves that way? A toddler."

"As if you've ever seen a toddler."

"There it is! That arrogance of a child. I did you a favor."

"By stripping me of my station?"

"That, you did that yourself. I am trying to understand why."

"You will never understand," Adrian seethed. The door juddered once more.

"Was it exile? Is that why you're here?"

"Do not disgrace me."

"Then perhaps you are right. I cannot wrap my mind around why any man would willingly submerge himself in such blatant misery."

Here, Adrian was quiet.

"I instructed you to work dawn til dusk, and yet you toil before morning every morning. I asked for large fruits and you have given me flowers that sever the clouds. You look as though a mudflat swallowed you whole, realized how foul you taste, and spat you back out. Why are you working yourself ragged?"

Nicholas nearly knocked his head in his haste to press his ear against the door.

"I am not strong enough."

He had to strain to hear it, but he was certain. He knew those words.

"Does that mean you plan to return when you are?"

"I...cannot."

"Why? Why force yourself away from a people you love so hopelessly you'd build a monument out of petals for them?"

"Because I don't know how to protect them!" The context wasn't exactly as Nicholas had imagined, but the picture was the same. He could see it through the wall: Malik's back pressed to the door, Adrian's arm shoved against his chest, a frown like a corkscrew.

"They are hunted by evil and they don't even realize. Nobody realizes except for me, nobody is willing to realize, and if I cannot reach them I have no right to- grace, even now I can feel it stalking, and I am ashamed. I will not return without the means to tear out its claws. And I won't accept criticism from a man who wouldn't understand duty if it slithered down his throat. You don't know the first thing about serving your people."

It was frantic bait. Malik let it sink into the water, ignored. "Then why aren't you chasing this evil? Hunt the hunter, do something."

"If I knew what to do it would be done!"

"Do something about that, too! Or do you plan to punish yourself here forever?" Malik waited, then went on, smug. "It is depressing, watching you wallow in your shame. It ruins my view. Do you know what's truly shameful? The only person you're saving from out here is yourself."

Another line straight off the page. Nicholas felt himself smile, knowing what came next.

"...Not to alarm you, but you're starting to sound worried."

Malik would be scowling now, a hint of a pout on his bottom lip. "My only concern is having my house back to myself as soon as possible."

"So what you're saying is, you want to help me?"

"Thank you. I nearly forgot I was speaking to a bull."

"Oh ye great sage, thou old hermit, do impart thy wisdom."

There was another thud. Nicholas wanted to run outside, to see Adrian grinning up from the ground and cry, open the book! Open it right now and believe me.

But if he inserted himself into the scene, would he change it? He was not a part of this story. A few words made fickle proof; what came next mattered more. There would be no denying him then. He had to be careful not to interfere.

"There is," Malik said, "or, there was- a seer. A witch in the walls of the old school, allowed to live comfortably so long as she devoted her life to Halcifer. She was bound to the castle by a powerful oath. And when the fighting broke out..."

Nicholas mouthed along to Adrian's words. "She was trapped."

"She lost her life, but I believe...well, from what I've read...I have a theory. That a shackled soul cannot be free even in death."

"A seer. You said foresight was impossible."

"It is. But there are other things to look for."

"To rely on witchcraft would be..."

"Unnatural? Look around you, Touro."

11. Halcifer School of Magic

A minute of privacy was too much to ask for, but all things considered, this was pretty okay. Steaming sun over his face, icy water curling over the rest of him, and the incomplete silence of the valley to keep him company.

"– and then he said, he said to me, that I ruined his goldenrods. I made them pink! There are scarce few things in this world that would be ruined by becoming pink. He is so– ungrateful!"

It was a very incomplete silence.

"Works me like an ox and then complains when I add a touch of myself, as if I'm not infused into every root, every cell of his ugly garden!"

"Mhm," droned Nicholas, drawing a sudsy rag over his chest. He thought the garden looked nice. Whatever Malik had made this soap from was decidedly pleasant.

"I'm going to– I'm going to– whither his foxgloves! He won't feel so big and bad then."

"Oh wow."

"Maybe I'll grind some into his dinner."

"Hmm."

"Are you even listening?" Adrian complained from deeper water, where he floated on his back with everything bared. Nicholas faced away. Apparently no one in this world had any hang-ups around nudity. "I just threatened to kill a man."

"Mhm," hummed Nicholas, and Adrian wailed.

"Count yourself lucky for that pretty face, stalker. I do not like to be ignored."

Nicholas ducked his burning cheeks beneath the water.

"I might just believe that rotten king made you his prisoner. At least that way I can blame it on trauma. You poor thing, he must have done a number on you."

Nicholas touched the raised scabs on his cheek where Yasmin's rings had cut him. They were, he realized, the only scars he'd taken away from the whole ordeal.

"Actually," Nicholas said, "he didn't do much at all."

Or at least he hadn't, until he sent Nicholas off under the pretense of release, only to bug his bag with an eavesdropping charm to monitor his every word. So much for the kindness of his heart, Nicholas thought resentfully.

Water rippled his way as Adrian shifted. "Wash my back," he said, very princely." When Nicholas was nearly behind him, he sheepishly added, "Please. Sorry." But Nicholas couldn't blame him. Malik had been working

Nicholas like a servant; veggies to be cooked, every corner of the house to be cleaned. With Adrian handling the garden and the hunt and Nicholas playing the housemaid, Malik was free to watch the entire day pass from his chair in the garden, the spitting image of the old recluse inside his soul.

"I'll tell you what he did," Adrian huffed at the first touch of the rag. He told Nicholas about things he already knew – the Interran ship that mysteriously sank right off the harbor, the severed beams that collapsed a terrane mine and killed nine of his people. The sickness that had been spreading, slowly but surely, through Interran cattle – the farmers called it a disease, diagnosable by the hot blush red that spread over the animal's tongue. But Adrian had found a crumpled petal near an infected pasture, and he'd scoured the archives for every book on poisons he could find. Charlatan's Oleander, a flower that only bloomed ruby red on the shore of the lake that bordered al-Narin.

"He will either kill us slowly or incite a war." Adrian spoke slow and short of breath. "Nobody believes me."

Nicholas already had his hands on Adrian's shoulders. So it was only natural, the placating squeeze of his fingers over the tight-wound muscle near the prince's neck. "I believe you."

Adrian sighed, at the touch or at the words. Nicholas studied the shades of Adrian's skin against his own, darker and so much richer. "A great comfort. The madman takes me seriously. Do that again."

Nicholas pressed his thumbs down, grateful for the cool balm of the river when Adrian gave a pleased hum.

"It is nice, though," Adrian said. "To have someone on my side. I won't take that for granted. Thank you, Nicholas. Again?"

Something crawled through Nicholas, the chill of the water. He had barely applied any pressure when Adrian wheeled around. Nicholas jumped, hands sliding down to his sides, as Adrian faced him with late-afternoon light striking his irises caramel brown. They were liquid, swirling angry, grasping, when he asked Nicholas, "Say it again. That you believe me."

Nicholas stammered, "I believe in you."

Adrian started to smile. "Changed the script a bit, there. Made it even sweeter. You'll stand with me, then?"

"I..."

"Say it. Please." Nicholas noted with a shudder that it was desperation in his voice, trembling his words like a bowstring. "That you'll help me. Stalker, spy, madman– whatever you are, it's alright. It's all alright. Just say it."

"I'm with you," Nicholas said on a torrid breath. "I'm with you."

The wild look in Adrian's eyes didn't ebb, but it took on a blunter edge. He gave in to the tug of his lips and his smile was a dangerous thing. "Are you flustered?"

Nicholas' voice came from the top of his throat. "You're very close."

Adrian glided back with a bow of his head that might've been apologetic, if Nicholas couldn't still see his smile afterward.

The journey to Halcifer lasted two full days and one night. Malik was reluctant to take on Nicholas' extra weight, but absolutely unwilling to leave him unsupervised anywhere near the house. He made his displeasure known often, though perhaps not as often as he could. Nicholas had Adrian to thank for that.

They fought. Frequently. Maybe always. Over the walking pace, over where to set up camp, over food rations, over the shapes of the clouds. Over what Adrian would say to the seer, if they could find her.

Nicholas spent much of the trip debating this last point, though of course he did so with less noise. They would find her. He would have to slip away once they were inside the school. If he didn't speak to her first, he wouldn't get a chance at all. But he needed to do it without altering the timeline, and–

He'd had a headache for two full days and one night just thinking about it. But in spite of the drumming between his eyeballs, the bickering, the urgent heat, the pain in both ankles the longer they walked, his sub zero stamina, all of the questions and none of the answers – he felt the first stroke of good fortune. He was on the very path he had set out for when he left Caldora, led by someone who knew the land by heart. And even if his travel companions didn't trust him yet, they were good people, and they were strong.

Though Adrian seemed to like him just fine.

He walked close, and he caught Nicholas' arm whenever Nicholas lost his footing, and in the breaths between his arguments with Malik, he kept smiling.

Nicholas was hesitant to observe this. On the second evening, they rested along the rocky river terrace, and Adrian sat cross-legged with his knee laid over Nicholas' thigh, and Nicholas hesitated. They ate the stretchy smoked meat of a boar that Adrian had caught with one of his flytraps and Nicholas had (poorly, nauseously) skinned. They refilled their canteens from a gravel bed where Malik deemed the water clean enough to drink. Adrian splashed sand onto Nicholas' neck, smiled, used his sleeve to wipe it away, and Nicholas hesitated.

A grumble sounded somewhere along the bank. Nicholas welcomed the distraction. He had learned the night before that the river wolves grew antsy near sundown, but he hardly even jumped this time. Malik seemed to know a trick to ward off every frontier beast. He sandwiched a small flute-shaped whistle between his lips and blew a soundless note. The growling instantly dropped away.

"If you're finished," he grunted, stomping out of the shallows with wet ankles and a deep scowl. His four braids jumped behind him as he marched onward, leaving their bags for Adrian and Nicholas to carry.

Minutes later, through a parting of trees, Halcifer came into view.

The ancient school was surprisingly...green. Later, when they got closer, the sun-bleached stone would show itself behind the moss, but from a distance it was as if Halcifer had gone into hiding. Six stories of jagged towers and turrets could hardly be camouflaged, though. Even overgrown and weathered down to dull tips, it stood tall as a king. Adrian straightened his spine.

"I take it you can make it the rest of the way without my help," Malik said when their feet struck stone, one long bridge from the huge oak doors. A final parting jab, but it lacked his usual scorn. He was staring at the walls, tracing over every edge like he couldn't help himself.

"Come off it," said Adrian. "You can't still want to go back."

"We agreed that I would guide you here and no further."

"It will be dangerous to travel alone."

Malik snorted. "I reckon I'll be safer without you halfwits." And he moved to leave, though his head turned slower than the rest of him, eyes lagging behind. Adrian took his wrist.

"Have you ever gone inside?"

"This place longs to sleep. I pity the fool who wakes it."

"Pity this fool to the door, then. What if the Mingles come for me on the bridge? I'll drown."

"Stupid bull."

Adrian took a step back, onto the first stone step up to the bridge. Malik shook off his grip but followed. Nicholas watched Adrian's eyes soften, so secretly fond he didn't even realize himself, and thought he had been right to hesitate. He laughed a little, embarrassed.

But Adrian offered his hand to Nicholas next. "As if I'd let you walk behind me, stalker." He grinned, and didn't drop his hand until they had crossed the river.

By the time they reached the doors, Malik didn't need convincing to go further. He had lost that fight with himself the second he stepped onto the bridge. He was the one to give the first push. The door didn't budge, so he put some magic into it, breathing in deep when the first gust of rich history hit his face.

"I lead," was his one rule as they stepped inside. "You listen."

"Yes, mother dear."

"I'll drown you myself, Touro."

The door closed loudly of its own weight behind them. Evening light wove past the weeds hanging over the windows. It bounced off of centuries-old shards of glass shattered around every sill, slippery beneath their feet. They stepped slowly over moth-eaten carpet in a massive, indistinguishable space – a scar, or maybe a wrinkle. It was impossible to tell whether the disarray was a relic of war or neglect.

"This place is..." said Adrian.

"Beautiful," Malik sighed.

"I was going to say 'haunting.'"

There was a deep, wet snarl.

"Haunted," amended Adrian.

Malik blew his whistle. The growling didn't stop but doubled, coming from either side. Malik tried his whistle again, again, shoulders rising with every failed blow.

Beneath opposite archways appeared two long-limbed, dog-like animals – if dogs walked on webbed paws; had short, watertight fur; and stood up to a grown man's chest. The river wolves gave strange gurgling growls and stalked closer. Adrian moved as if to run. Malik gripped the back of his shirt and whispered around the whistle, "Don't be an idiot."

Slowly, he knelt. He lay his palm to the ground, over a patch of carpet that had been eaten away to reveal stone.

The first wolf lunged, and Malik pulled, drawing a stone cudgel straight from the floor. It collided with the wolf's side with a crunch that made Nicholas' stomach roll. Then Nicholas was toppling to the floor, shoved out of harm's way as the second wolf howled and leapt. Adrian took the weight of the pounce and managed, as he fell, to twist his hands like he was drawing rope. The vines shrouding one window snaked into the fight, wrapping around the wolf's neck to pull its head back just before blood-stained teeth could plunge into his throat. Adrian clenched his fists, twisted; the vines wrenched one way and the wolf's neck snapped ninety degrees.

It kept snarling, gnashing its teeth sideways. The first wolf stood. Its front leg bowed the wrong way and for a moment, it teetered. Then it adjusted. Then it began to walk.

Adrian scrambled backward, into Nicholas. "These are..." he trailed.

Up close, it was obvious. Their black fur was matted with blood. The first was covered in enough deep gashes to slowly, painfully bleed it out. The second had his throat torn open. Their eyes were colorless, filled with dark fluid.

This time, Malik was on the same page. "They're dead," he said. "They killed each other."

Nicholas didn't have any right to be shocked. He had designed them. But no amount of expectation could stave off the fear, an order of fear he had never experienced– hadn't even had the room for, in his cushy earthly life.

"Don't move," Adrian ordered breathlessly, which was great, because Nicholas wasn't confident he could.

The first wolf came charging again. Malik's cudgel collided with its head this time. It staggered, reared up, and slammed its front legs into his chest. Adrian shouted and ran to help him, then shouted again – the second wolf had pulled free of the vines and latched onto his boot.

"Focus on yourself!" said Malik. Liquid oozed from the wolf's indented skull onto his cheek. He gripped the cudgel in both hands, barring the wolf's snapping maw as far from his face as his arms allowed. Then he yanked his hands apart, suddenly holding two stone daggers.

Adrian furiously shook his foot. When that didn't work, he tried to haul the wolf off with vines tangled around its ankles, its neck, its snout. They tore under the pressure. Malik stabbed everywhere he could reach, narrowly avoiding claws and teeth.

There was an agonized yowl that petered into a whine. The first wolf lurched, half its body sagging, tongue lolling out of its mouth as it floundered for footing.

"Aim for the eyes!" yelled Malik, driving his other blade home. The wolf went limp on top of him.

Adrian's vines had thickened enough to hold the beast in place. Nicholas knew better than to keep watching but watched nonetheless as two tendrils dove into the gash in the wolf's neck. Seconds later, they burst out through its eye sockets, and the beast stilled.

Adrian lowered himself and leaned off some of his weight against Nicholas' side. "You're shaking. Are you hurt?"

The room reeked of blood and rot. Nicholas convulsed, tightening his throat to hold back vomit. "You're asking me?"

"Coward," Malik panted. He leered over Nicholas. "There were two of them and three of us. If you don't plan to make yourself useful–"

"Easy," said Adrian. "What would you have him do? He is powerless."

It was a simple truth. Adrian hadn't said it to insult him. And yet the words struck Nicholas in the chest and left a dent – easy, probably, when the space was so hollow. They were too true, and had been that way for too long.

Adrian scrounged together an almost-smile. "Are you going to tell me all of that was in your book?"

"Oh. Um. Not all–"

"There are bigger issues here than your fucking book," Malik snapped. He crouched before Adrian and smacked his boot. "Off."

The bite marks hadn't made it too deep into his foot. While Malik cleaned the wound and dressed it with ointment, Adrian touched his ankle and focused hard. Slowly, the edges of the punctures crept together. By the pained scrunch to his face as he stood, he hadn't healed it all the way down. "Too slow," he grunted at Malik's dubious look.

There were archways leading out of the room in every direction. Malik picked one, seemingly at random, but no one questioned him. "There is sick magic at work here," he said, pausing over the fallen body of his wolf. "What kind of twisted sadist would desecrate their rest?"

"At least we know our witch is here," sneered Adrian. He didn't look happy. He knelt at each wolf's side in turn and muttered something. Nicholas caught the tail end of a prayer, and peace to your soul.

They walked the ruined hallways as the sunlight waned. Sometimes there was rustling or scuttling, and all three of them would tense, but whatever creatures had made the abandoned school their home kept themselves hidden. Malik led them up one set of stairs, then another. A rotting step gave way beneath Nicholas' feet. Adrian caught him under the shoulders and hauled him onto his step, and only let go when the paralyzed-deer look faded from Nicholas' eyes.

"You're okay," Adrian assured him.

"Why are you being so nice to me?"

Adrian tested the weight of the next closest step, hopped to it, and beckoned. "I will be mean if I have to. I don't know who decided distrust should be the default."

They entered a grand room with a fresco ceiling and mosaic floor. The greatest parties in Maesia had probably taken place where they stood, but now the art seemed ghoulish. Above them, hundreds of children in ancient drapes danced, their hands overflowing with precious stones. Below, fire, water, and earth twisted from the hands of mages, the very first.

"What's got you so antsy?" said Malik, less a question of concern than a demand that Nicholas stop fidgeting in his peripherals.

Then the ceiling caved in.

The chubby, blushing faces of the dancing children rained down. With the forcate on his middle finger, Malik diverted a chunk that would have knocked him unconscious – or dead – and did the same for Adrian. But there were too many. He gave up on fighting and ran. That was when the ground began to crumble.

Malik did his best, deflecting stones above them and trying to hold the tile beneath, but his power could only stretch so far. He and Adrian wound up backing up, tripping in the direction they had come.

And Nicholas, who had stood across from them when the floor first cracked, had no choice but to run the opposite way.

"Nicholas!" Adrian shouted, stopping, despite everything, to reach across the growing gap between them. Malik yanked him by the back of the shirt an instant before the floor he stood on gave way.

"You'll get us all killed," said Malik. Adrian looked at Nicholas for a moment longer, distraught, and Nicholas felt that in his chest, too, though it was a different, less familiar sort of ache. How long had it been since he'd made a friend?

Nicholas stumbled on shifting ground, barely one step ahead of the collapse. The destruction caught up to him and he pitched forward, aiming for the sturdy wood floor at the outskirts of the room.

He missed. And he fell.

Reaching wildly, his hand smacked onto something thick and brown. He wrapped his fingers tight around a branch of the ivy crawling up the wall, engorged to the size of his wrist. It only held his weight for a few seconds, but it was long enough to sling his other arm onto the floor above. He towed himself up and crumpled, panting, at the edge of the room, his back to a door.

There was a gaping hole in the ceiling where the fresco had been. The chasm in the floor was exactly circular, a perfect cutout of the fallen mosaic. Across it were Malik and Adrian, slumped against the other entrance. There was no way to cross.

Nicholas didn't have the breath to say thank you, but he thought, as Adrian met his eye and nodded, that he didn't need to. Nicholas nodded, too, setting his jaw, eyes hard and determined. I'll find my way.

12. The Curse of the Faisans

Nicholas made eye contact with a marble bust on a podium and bowed his head in a way he hoped came off more deferent than dismissive. There wasn't time to worry about it. He navigated the halls quickly, all too aware he was racing against two tough, athletic, magic-wielding men. Malik had the advantage of encaline, the charmstone; it would lead him directly to the powerful charm that anchored the seer to Halcifer. Nicholas had the advantage of the shortest path and the journal in his hands.

In the chaos of the cave in, he had leaned into his own clumsiness, letting himself be jostled and thrown around as the ceiling rained over them. Malik, who had adamantly carried Nicholas' work bag (and not much else) throughout their journey, was in that moment too focused on surviving to notice Nicholas crashing into his side, let alone the hand diving into the bag's pocket. With a well-timed stumble, Nicholas had placed himself across the center of the mosaic just as the first fractures appeared in the tile.

Now, walking alone through a darkening castle with eyes in its walls, he contemplated hubris. He ducked every time he glimpsed a portrait frame, but many of them were faceless, washed out by the sun or destroyed by wind, rain, and alarmingly, claws. Three flights of stairs, two unfortunate bladder movements (for an abandoned castle, there really were a lot of noises), and one curved door later, he stood at the entrance to a tiny, hexagonal library.

He noticed, inching back into the doorway, that the paintings on these walls had hardly faded. There were no windows, only a stained-glass ceiling that probably didn't let in much sun in broad daylight; so close to dusk, the room was nearly dark. The walls and shelves were wrapped in crawling plants that shouldn't have been able to grow here. The floor was almost completely hidden - by more vines, but also cracking clay sculptures, tarnished statues, suits of armor, dolls, bones. Anything with eyes, or at least a space for them.

Nicholas let the door fall. Fighting the urge to check that it hadn't somehow locked behind him, he cleared his throat and said, "Hello? Miss Dalisay?"

The granite wall opposite him was carved in the likeness of a fair, strict woman from the shoulders up. It was a dedication to Halcifer's first headmistress, but Nicholas supposed that wasn't stated anywhere in the journal. For all he knew, in this version of things he was looking at Dalisay. He opted for that, if only for somewhere to aim his supplicating smile.

"You snuck in."

Nicholas whipped to his left and faced the seer. The witch, apparently, even if he hadn't written her that way (though, when he thought about it, he may have not written her any way at all. Maybe this was how the journal had filled the empty space around her existence, by creating a new branch of magic altogether).

She peered down at him from the portrait of a later, grayer headmaster. Its mouth moved when she spoke, its long beard dipping in and out of frame. "You snuck in. Tell me how, tell me how, tell me why I did not feel you, tell me why I can see you but I still cannot feel you, tell me how!"

Her voice wasn't so much a voice but the rustle of the vines along the walls, the scraping of metal against the shelves, the scattering of skeletal paws over the floor. Yet somehow the sound came directly from the painting's mouth, and somehow every syllable rang clear, and somehow he heard her in it, the witch, the woman.

"I'm...not sure. Sorry. But- it could be," said Nicholas, "I don't have any magic."

"Everybody has magic." Nicholas spun again, this time staring up at a portrait of a ghoulish old headmistress. "It is woven into the earth, fool, and our flesh is born from the earth, fool."

"Not mine." Nicholas held up the book for her to see. There was an unsettled swishing as the floor shifted. "I would like to ask, um, humbly, that you lend me your sight. Ma'am."

The statues, the dolls, the carcasses - all of it began to stand, like a wave rolling over the floor.

"How dare you," she hissed, her voice jumping rapidly from portrait to portrait, centuries of headmasters, until Nicholas was dizzy. "How dare you, how dare you, how dare you!"

He tried to step back toward the door and nearly lost his balance as vines slithered underfoot.

"Is every man from every universe rotten?" A fangy skull gnashed its teeth, a suit of armor bashed its fist against a bookshelf. "What do I owe? Why must

I see for you? It is not my fault you are all as dumb and blind as kittens, you kitten, you pitiful kitten, haven't I done enough?"

A tiny skeleton on four legs nipped at Nicholas' ankle with pinprick teeth. Nicholas had to grab a shelf for footing as Dalisay wailed.

"I think I can help you."

The floor shuddered, grumbled, and stilled. "What do you mean?"

"It isn't just that I have no magic, it's like...I'm so magicless that I cancel magic. My hands, my skin..." To prove it, he bent over and pulled his socks low, so the skeleton at his feet bit his bare ankle and slumped. The room murmured. He withdrew his foot and it clambered onto its paws.

"If I touch the talisman and release its magic, even for a second..."

"Would you really?" asked Dalisay from the mouth of a cloth doll with button eyes. The skeleton arched its spine warily. "You would free me, would you?"

"Yes," Nicholas said, tight in the throat because he knew he wouldn't get the chance.

The skeleton trotted over to Nicholas' other foot and stretched its head, rubbing its cheek against his ankle. It began to purr.

"Oh!" she cried. "I was a child, you know, when they took me, and only so much older when the fighting began. And now, how long have I been young? Was I ever truly young, if I've only been young in this room? How long have I been dead? You must be an angel - or a reaper, oh, I will take either, any, if I may leave this place!"

The floor rippled outward in all directions as the junk cleared itself from the center of the room, scuttling toward the walls to reveal a raised circular dais inscribed with runes.

"Come," said Dalisay. "Where I can see you."

Nicholas stepped onto the dais, careful not to touch the object at its center. There, still standing upright after centuries, was a scale welded intricately from bronze and glass. It curved along the stem like a wise old tree, holding up matching round trays with the chains dangling from its branches.

"Do you see the irony? They lectured me about balance. And then they killed each other."

A mud-colored crystal was inlaid at the junction between the branches, unremarkable save for the way it popped and hissed, crackling with bare-ly-held energy. The more significant the object, the more powerful a charm it could hold. For a feat so impossible as binding a body and soul for life, only an impossible talisman would do. The ugly brown gem on the scale was made of all nine kova zem, altogether.

"I don't know how to get home," said Nicholas.

The woman in the granite wall closed her eyes, then opened her mouth to speak. Dalisay looked into his past and said, "You have been alone a long time, have you, Nicholas?"

He made a sound like he'd been punched. But he nodded.

"How long do you feel you've been alive?"

Nicholas hesitated. The wording was strange, but...

"Seven years."

At least, the first seven years of his life were the only ones he truly felt he'd lived. That seemed to appease her.

"You had a lot to say once, when you were very young. Do you remember?"

He shook his head.

"What a shame, what a shame. Such a sweet voice you had, all those years ago."

She moved on to his present. "Oh! You know a witch, how delightful."

"I don't."

"That book you hold. Perhaps it wears another name where you come from, but here we call it witchcraft. Sorcery for the cultured few. She gave you a wonderful gift, I do hope you thank her."

"Gift?" Nicholas spluttered. "This thing ruined my life."

"History cannot be undone, only destroyed and rewritten."

Those were Cici's word's. He had heard them too many times to forget.

"What? Wait, how do you-"

The carving's eyes flew open. Nicholas had to hop to avoid the vines swarming the dais, steered by their olive-shaped flowers - brown with seeds at the center, white and red on every petal, like bloodshot eyes. They curled atop the dais, slowly taking shape.

Dalisay's next words echoed off the walls. "Tread heavily. Look behind you. If you fear fire, learn to harden your skin; you will burn with every step-"

Her booming voice dropped away. The image drawn on the dais was only fully formed for a second before the vines recoiled with a whistling sound, and every figure littering the floor reared onto its haunches. Moments later, Adrian barreled through the door.

"You're here! Saints, we were so worried." He threw his arms around Nicholas. Between the two of them, he looked worse for wear. "Well, mainly I was, but you know Malik, he hides well."

"You're with the Faisan," snarled Dalisay, everywhere at once. The floor surged in on Adrian, an army of animated bodies stalking toward him in tides. They had him encircled before he could press his back to the door.

Nicholas threw himself from the dais and into harm's way. The attack came to a growling hault, and Adrian murmured from behind him, "What the hell do you think you're doing?"

"Don't hurt him. Remember our deal? I'll keep up my end, but you can't hurt him."

Nicholas made up his mind that he meant it, all of it. Even if the journal wouldn't perfectly match up. He had enough proof. Dalisay didn't have to suffer for his sake.

"You formed a pact with this wretch?" sneered Adrian. "Well then tell your friend to stop attacking mine. Leave him be! We came peacefully - Malik has done nothing to you!"

Anger rolled through the room, so bright Nicholas could see it in the empty sockets and lifeless eyes surrounding them. "Do you even know?" asked the walls. "Do you know? Do you have any idea? Have you any knowledge of your history, wretch? Or will it shock you to learn who chained me here? I can feel him, I can feel his magic!"

Nicholas watched it dawn on Adrian - the immense power of the Faisans, their command over encaline. The fact that Malik did know his history, and was too smart not to have anticipated the target on his back, and had come anyway.

"Malik had nothing to do with that. He's fighting for his life out there."

"You do not know a grudge until you've been half-dead hundreds of years, boy."

"You chose to serve Halcifer."

"It was that or die! If I had been any older, I may have chosen death. Tell me, were you ever handed a noose as a child?"

Adrian glanced at the door. When he turned back, his eyes had hardened to stone.

"Fine," he said, bowing his head. "I...apologize. Forgive me. Please allow me to use your eyes."

"What will you offer in return?"

"My friend."

The walls cackled. The dais cleared again. Adrian stepped onto it. He held his chin high, but he looked unsteady.

"I need..." he rasped. He looked to Nicholas. "Can you come here?" Nicholas moved to the edge of the dais, but Adrian pleaded, "Closer."

Any closer might disrupt her sight. Nicholas did what he could, reaching out his hand. Adrian grasped it tight enough to hurt, and didn't let go until the carving in the wall had closed its eyes.

"You miss your father deeply, don't you?"

Adrian didn't react until the silence had stretched on too long. Only when he said, "Every day," the corners of his mouth drawn tight, did Dalisay continue.

"You miss your mother as well, although she is still with you. But then, is she?"

"She is," Adrian snapped. The floor began to groan. The woman on the wall's mouth twitched downward, eyes fluttering. Adrian retreated toward the middle of the dais as bony claws began to scrape at its rim. "No," he wheezed. "No, she isn't. She's been gone a long time."

The room settled.

"What have you felt since?"

"I've been...sad, of course. But I'm trying my best."

The floor rustled. "What have you felt the most?" Dalisay demanded.

Through clenched teeth, Adrian admitted, "Bitterness."

Then, the present. "One dead, one good as dead. Instead of taking their place, you have fled Sigla Palace to drown in your incompetence and...oh, what is that? Ambition. So great an ambition you do not know what to do with yourself. It has taken everything within you to hold it back, you poor, valiant boy. You take it upon yourself to carry all the world, don't you?"

This was not a question Adrian had to answer, but he nodded anyway.

Her eyes shot wide. The vines began to move. The force of Adrian's fortune was so great, her voice rattled the shelves. "Dig through the sands of Lake Charlatan for the poison you seek. Pull it up by the root and possess it, or else cut it at the stem and watch it bloom twice as bright."

Nicholas recognized the shape on the dais. He had seen those oleander bushes in his dream.

"What does that mean?" said Adrian. "What does any of that mean?"

If there was an answer, they wouldn't get to hear it. The room trembled with rage as Malik appeared in the doorway.

He brandished a long metal bat, but it looked heavy in his grip. He stood lopsided, panting with his whole body and bruised all over. His pants and his sleeves were in shreds. A despairing whine came from Adrian's throat.

"And there you are, you devil, you prize!"

Nicholas understood then that Dalisay had never really been attacking before. When the floor rushed at Malik this time, there was no getting away.

Empty armor drew its sword and nearly took Malik's head. Malik swung at the helmet and dented the eye slits; it fell away. But then there was a figurine stabbing at his ankles, and a winged carcass soaring at his head, and a bronze cougar snapping at his thighs, and he could only do so much. Adrian raised his hands to control the vines and blanched when he found he couldn't. They were under the witch's control. A marble bust slammed a wheeze from Malik's chest.

Adrian yelled. The door flew off its hinges as huge, sharp-tipped roots shot into the room from who-knew-how-far. They curled around Malik, snakelike and fiercely protective, swatting and spearing the assailants.

Nicholas lunged for the talisman. The vines shifted beneath his feet and he tripped painfully backward onto his tailbone. They were hurtling for Malik, winding tight around his shins and climbing higher. The other attacks went limp as Dalisay poured all of her magic into rapid mummification.

"Have you forgotten? We made a pact! I know all about pacts! Come, little Faisan, learn how it feels to be trapped."

Malik turned terrified eyes onto Adrian, betrayed.

As the vines climbed around his shoulders, one of the roots twisted around Malik's wrist and yanked, extending his arm far enough for Adrian's outstretched hand to wrap around the bat.

"Wait!" shouted Nicholas. The swarming vines raced over his hands and feet, dragging him down as he tried to stand, just shy of the dais.

The walls shrieked, "You swore! You swore, you swore!"

But Adrian's oath had not been bound by magic. He brought the bat down on the scale with all of his might, over and over until the corpses stopped twitching and the vines went listless. Adrian hauled Malik into an embrace. After a moment, Malik pressed quivering hands to Adrian's back. Dalisay died a second time, still too trusting, betrayed by mages until the very end.

"It is not your duty to mourn her," said Adrian when the dust had settled, joining Nicholas at the edge of the dais. "She was wicked. She was a monster."

"She was lonely."

Adrian hugged Nicholas against his side. Nicholas didn't understand how touch came so effortlessly for him, how he never shied away from the impulse. Nicholas dared to lean onto his shoulder. The world didn't shake, but he did, a little.

Malik sat before them. "This bag has been feeling a bit light," he said, looking pointedly at the book in Nicholas' hands.

"Ah, yeah. I had my own questions."

"You knew exactly how this would unfold." He didn't have the energy to sound angry about it. "Did you get your answers?"

"I ran out of time."

"I stole your chance," realized Adrian, rough with remorse.

"And you?" said Malik. Adrian recited Dalisay's final words. "Does she mean the flower, the charlatan's oleander- the one that poisoned the cattle?"

"It can't be," said Adrian.

"Too straightforward." Malik smiled wearily. "Spirits forbid anything comes easy."

"I think I understand," said Adrian, looking anything but relieved. "It seems my time has finally come to meet the king of Caldora." With a dark chuckle, he added, "Think you can introduce us?"

Before she was interrupted, Dalisay had told Nicholas that he was going to burn. And the image in the vines - the short glimpse he'd gotten - he was pretty sure he had seen a roaring, all-consuming flame. The thought of returning to Caldora, to Rayan and his fire, now every bit the enemy he'd suspected, sent Nicholas keeling forward to hold his face in his hands.

"Hey, now," Adrian nudged. "Only joking. You don't have to come."

"I said I'd stand by you."

"Oh," said Adrian on a sharp breath out. "You can do that from anywhere, darling. Don't risk your life for me." To Malik, he said, "And you...I suppose we will say goodbye here, too."

"Don't be an idiot. You won't even make it out of the frontier without my help."

Through exhausted eyes and a busted lip, Adrian beamed.

Nicholas had nowhere else to go, and his one lead was off in the ether. Adrian was the only comfort within reach, his only shot at help. He latched on. And, besides,

"You want to see the book, don't you?"

He opened it in his lap, turned it around for the others to read. They didn't look surprised, exactly, as they parsed the pages. They'd known what to expect - the only thing left was to believe it. Adrian's face slowly went slack, and Malik's turned frighteningly neutral.

The door opened. Adrian was on his feet in an instant, placing himself in front of Malik and Nicholas. Nicholas heard all of his breath leave him.

"What did you do to her?" said a new voice. Nicholas leaned just so to see past Adrian's knees. The girl in the doorway was one he knew - and one who did not belong in this part of the story. Tall, dark, and glittering gold stood the second heir to the Interran throne.

13. Fool's Game

Amara's hood had fallen away. She had a long, straight body, exposed by the open front of her cloak. Her shirt was tight and cropped just beneath her chest. She wore two braids tight to her skull, woven from the crown of her head to her middle back. Gold glittered at her nose, hung from her navel, crawled up her ears and dangled from the lobes.

She said again, "What did you do to her?"

"What did I do? Why are you here?" Adrian stormed to the doorway. They stood at nearly the same height, yet he scowled down at her. "How did you get here?"

"Dalisay," said Amara. "Where is she? What did you do—"

"She is gone!" He threw an arm behind him. When Amara saw the destroyed talisman, her hand came over her mouth. "Now would you care to explain—"

"You killed her."

Adrian pulled at his own cheeks as if holding onto his sanity. "She was already dead. If anything, I released her."

"No!" cried Amara. She ran to the dais and dropped to her knees. "No, no– she wanted only to rest, but you've gone and destroyed her tether, and now..." She touched the shattered glass. Blood welled from her fingertip. She hardly seemed to notice Nicholas or Malik sitting feet away. Close up, Nicholas could see the dust on her cloak, in her hair. "She will drift."

Broken glass, a broken deal; that was some nasty symbolism. Maybe it wasn't his duty, maybe the only good it did was assuage his own guilt, but Nicholas would mourn the witch nonetheless.

"It was her life or ours," said Adrian. "Would you have preferred–"

"Stop that," she said with a fierce glare.

"Amara."

"I had to prove it, to myself and everyone. That my brother is alive."

"How did you find me?"

"I felt you. I was following that feeling, but then there was something else, and it pulled." Her hand grasped at nothing in front of her chest. "It pulled me here."

"What do you mean you could feel me?" Her glossing eyes cleared as she watched him approach, unmoved by his tone. "How long have you been here?"

"I...don't know."

"You don't–? Did you come alone?"

"As if I would have been allowed otherwise."

"What were you thinking? These are not harmless lands."

"I was thinking that the asinine search parties making laps around the kingdom would sooner get themselves lost than find you. And someone had to find you."

"You could have gotten yourself killed!"

"I am not helpless!" She stood with her chin raised and her hand at her hip, where the hilt of a sword peeked past her cloak. With each aggravated rise and fall of her chest, the branches inked along her ribs wavered as if swaying in the wind. Adrian's jaw was set so tight, he might actually have been biting his tongue. Because, despite her perfect breeding, despite the four stones cuffed around her arms, Amara's magic was so weak it may as well not have been there at all.

"And who have you left in charge?" Adrian demanded.

"The same man who has been in charge since mama lost her mind," she bit.

"Don't you speak of her that way."

"It's the damned truth! And here, another – Regent Mava would have finally been relieved of his provisional role had someone not run off into the skies the morning of his coronation!"

Adrian sent a panicked look Malik's way. Malik, for his part, looked unimpressed.

"None of this–" Malik waved a hand vaguely, "–has been subtle, Your Highness."

Adrian didn't get time to process that. Amara shoved against his chest with enough strength to nearly drop him. "I cannot believe you ran off to...to...what are you even doing? What could be so important that you should abandon our people?"

"And what do you call what you've done?" said Adrian. "At least I did not leave them alone."

"At least I left a note. Would that have been so hard, to let us know?"

Her voice broke. She turned away from him.

Adrian crossed the space between them and pulled her against him. Amara pushed her face, still drawn tight in a glower, into the crook of his neck.

"I didn't want the asinine search parties on my scent," he said. "I forgot to plan for my asinine little sister."

She shrugged her arms around him like she was reluctant to do so, but she held tight.

"I apologize," said Adrian. He yelped as Amara pinched his side.

"Not good enough."

"...Fair."

After a heavy moment, she asked, "Really, brother. What are you doing?"

He shook his head. "Tomorrow. For now, let us rest."

Halcifer probably would have been the safest place to spend the night, but the decision was made unanimously, and with no words passed between them, to leave. The quietness followed them across the bridge. Though he tried to hide it, Malik walked with a limp. Nicholas had drawn Adrian's guilt enough times to recognize it on his face – Malik had fought hard so that Adrian could go on, and Adrian seemed intent on punishing himself for this, because he didn't look away. On the other side of the river, Malik blew his whistle against the wolves and led them deeper into the brush. He and Adrian summoned branches, dirt, and stone to make a hut. They chewed on smoked meat and ate their nuts unroasted. No one had the energy for a fire.

The next morning, Nicholas explained his situation again, this time to believing ears. Amara accepted it all with unexpected readiness. She listened and watched, and when it was over, she touched the journal's cover with gold-banded fingers and said, "This is beautiful."

"Terrifying is what it is." Adrian had a grudging look to him, a petulant sort of aggravation. "My fate is in these pages."

"Shall we see what it holds?" said Malik.

When the journal lay bared between them, Amara said, "Your art is lovely."

It was the first time she had addressed Nicholas directly. She smiled, and he remembered belatedly to thank her. Four heads leaned over the open pages. Adrian snapped early on for Malik to stop turning them so quickly. Malik made a jab at Adrian's intelligence. After that, it was quiet, only the occasional affected noise when they saw their exact words shouted back at them. Amara looked away once they arrived at Dalisay's death. Malik quickly flipped past, into what hadn't yet come to be.

Malik mumbled a curse. Amara, a prayer.

"You have to change this," Adrian said. "Rewrite it."

His frown had taken on a deep set. Nicholas rummaged through his bag for a pencil.

Adrian's patience wore quickly as Nicholas rubbed at the paper. "What are you doing?"

"Trying to erase it."

"It isn't working. Why isn't it working?"

Nicholas tried to imagine looking into his own future and seeing his failure sketched in bold. With an attempt at gentleness, he said, "I'm not sure."

"So cross it out!" Adrian cleared his throat. "Draw over it, or– try something. Anything else."

So Nicholas did try. He flipped his pencil around and dragged a line in the corner of the page, as a test. Nothing happened. He scratched the pencil against the knee of his pants. It left an ashy line. Back to the page again; nothing.

"Press harder."

Sketched in graphite were Adrian and Malik, diving away from Caldoran flames into the waters of Lake Charlatan. It was a narrow escape, a lucky break. Depending on how you looked at it, a shamefaced retreat.

Nicholas pressed harder.

"Tear out the page," Adrian urged. Amara touched his shoulder, but he shrugged her off. "Try."

Nicholas did not want to tear out his work. But he did try, just a little, at the very top. The paper clung to the bindings. Adrian swatted his hand away, held the book down, and pulled so hard his muscles drew taut. The page did not come away. With a frustrated shout, he jumped to his feet, sending the book sprawling.

"Adrian!" scolded Amara. She reached forward, but Malik beat her to the book. He tucked it onto his lap and continued through the pages in private. "Adrian," she said again, softer. He paced with his hands over his head, visibly grinding his teeth. "It is still your story. Rewrite it yourself."

"I say you try for an official audience," offered Malik. "Rather less threatening than appearing on his doorstep."

"What is it you think I was doing on his doorstep?" Adrian gestured angrily to the book. "Or, will do– am doing– dammit! And I have tried to be subtle. Patience, diplomacy, I have tried it endlessly. Do you know how difficult it is to get a letter to the king of an unfriendly nation? We meet at the harbors, is that right?"

Adrian made scalding reference to the only amiable agreement still standing between their kingdoms. In the interest of trade, all acrimony was forgotten in the waters of the southernmost Caldoran port city and the northernmost Interran harbor.

"I have sent men to the ports, I have thrown coins at worthless traders on the scarce hope one of them may have the right connections. I have taken ships myself and loitered and peddled and begged– me, a prince! And I know he has seen my writing, I know, because I have spoken to many a high-standing merchant, men with lineages so old I can find their names in Interran texts. And never a word back!"

He threw his hands up, but he didn't drop them. He stopped in place and followed them with his eyes, baring his face to the watery sun. When he turned, dropping his arms heavily as if he had just let go of something burdensome, there was resolution in his gaze, and defiance unbefitting a prince.

"If I want to be heard, I will have to be loud. I must go to him."

Slowly, he began to smile, but it was different than before. Meaner. This boy was too big to fit on a page and too vigorous to sit still inside a book, but God, Nicholas wanted to try. If he got the chance to put pen to paper again, he would do Adrian justice.

"But we lose this fight," Malik said, only half paying attention.

"So we'll do things differently!" Adrian had come alive. "A poison grown from the sands of Lake Charlatan. That has to be him. I must grab him by the root before he incites a war–"

Malik slammed the book shut. Pink bloomed along the tips of his ears.

"What is it?" said Adrian. "What did you see?"

"Nothing. Just...an insect."

"You, flinching at an insect?" Adrian chuckled. "Impossible."

He bent forward to investigate. Malik pushed the journal into the bag and stood. "We should leave," he said. "Maximize our daylight."

Amara rose as well, looking in all parts ready for a fight. "The Caldoran is right."

Adrian grabbed her by the hood. "We will leave. You need to go home."

Her eyes flashed. "You can't seriously–"

"You have always been more suited to lead than I," said Adrian. He did not soften his tone, though his eyes crinkled full of fondness. "So lead. Mava is wonderful at his job, but he must feel deeply lost. One of us needs to be there, and it cannot be me. I have to..."

"I understand," said Amara. "I read every word."

"I need you to return as though you never found me."

"I need you to return."

"I swear I will."

"Then I swear my silence."

She took off her cloak and clasped it around his collar. When she stood with her sword visible, hanging long and heavy in its sheath, she looked for the first time exactly as Nicholas had envisioned. Graceful, brave. Conscious of her own weakness and stronger for it.

She turned without a farewell. "Be safe," Adrian called out by way of goodbye. She turned over her shoulder and poked her tongue at him, and the image shattered.

When she disappeared through the trees, Adrian shrugged his shoulders rather anticlimactically and said, "Last chance to call it a day and return to your peace." When no one said anything, he grinned. "No takers? You're all fools."

As far as enemy territory infiltrations went, this one involved little fanfare. There was no official boundary between the kingdoms, no border guard. Just a wild frontier to cross and enough bad blood spilled to discourage wanderers. Still, Nicholas thought, there had to be wanderers. He wondered how many before them had made the trip, and how many had stayed wherever they landed.

Traversing the valley wall was considerably slower when he wasn't dragged by the ankle. With flat palms and fingers bared, Adrian summoned the stone buried beneath layers of earth to the surface, and Malik molded it into flat, wide steps. It was slow work, but Nicholas didn't want to imagine the climb without it. Still, by the end he was more sweat than human, and so sore in his calves he wobbled at the precipice and nearly tumbled back down. Adrian pulled him over the ledge and into his chest.

"Hard work looks good on you," he said. So the prince was a liar.

They made it to the Borderturf as the sun sank. Adrian paid for a closet of a room that reeked of rat piss with a tiny leaf-shaped stud from his ear. It probably could have bought out the whole inn, but he refused Nicholas' offer of Cairo's malon.

With another earring, carved after the sun, he secured a ride in a wooden wagon with uneven wheels. The driver and the donkey were equally thin. Adrian was already poor at hiding his discomfort surrounded by poverty, but at the sight of the breaths heaving beneath the beast's ribs as it struggled with their weight, his fidgeting turned to angry stewing that lasted the whole ride through. Without his chattiness, the wagon was stifling. It didn't help that in order to fit, Nicholas had to sit nearly on top of him, squished against the low wall. Adrian grabbed him around the back to stop him from toppling over the side at a rough bump so many times, he eventually just left his arm there.

Which was fine.

Nicholas was self-regulating just fine.

He had a long history of buckling easily, with the slightest pressure. A few wayward glances from a cute boy would do, the attention was a good feeling. He had given up all of his firsts to that feeling.

He wasn't that kid anymore, but Adrian made him feel dangerously young.

They left the wagon in the first reasonable city. Adrian gave up an opal stud for a humble carriage where they could all sit comfortably. With the donkey replaced by a healthy, if unnattractive horse, they rode in comfort.

Malik muttered something to the driver when they reached South Simona. The carriage stopped a while later in front of a square building with tall white columns.

Malik ignored any questions as he climbed out and ordered Adrian to stay put when he automatically started to follow. "You stand out like a sore thumb. The shurta will not miss that," Malik said with his voice lowered, nodding to the officers stationed at the doors.

He reappeared nearly an hour later, shadowed by a short man with pudgy hands clasped beneath an unctuous smile. It took another five minutes for Malik to shake the man off, and he returned with a put-upon huff and a bag full of cash.

Adrian gawked. "Where did you get that?"

"The bank," Malik said simply. Adrian reached up as if to strangle him or kiss him. Malik showed off the ring on his left middle finger. Unlike the jewelry on his right, it had a flat, ovular face with no gem. A stamp was carved into the surface, an emblem picturing a fire-spitting bird with three wings. "You of all people should understand the value of a name."

"Fox!" Adrian laughed, grabbing Malik's hand to take a closer look.

"Bull," Malik grumbled, snatching his hand back, though he failed to hide that he was pleased. Nicholas looked away.

Malik told the driver to take them to the nearest ready-made tailor. He allowed Adrian along this time (after plentiful whining), and all three of them walked out in new clothing. Adrian pulled uncomfortably at the tight seams and whined some more. Nicholas was baking beneath a loose coat that reached his calves, but he suffered in silence.

There were no more stops after that. The next evening, nestled in the plush cushions of an outrageously pricey carriage, they arrived at al-Narin's outermost gate.

It went as it had in the original story. The king's shurta crossed their spears over the gate. Malik approached and introduced himself by name. Nicholas and Adrian were his men. He showed his ring.

The gates opened. One guard escorted them deeper alongside the driver.

The same introduction, this time at an inner gate. They were handed off to another guard and led on foot a shorter distance down the paved path, to yet another gate.

"These gardens," Malik commented, looking from left to right to study both sides of the path.

"The late queen was very knowledgeable about flora," said the guard, stonefaced. "Our king makes great effort to keep her passion alive."

Adrian snorted and hid it behind a cough. Muffled by the traditional headdress wrapped over his forehead and nose, it was believable enough.

The great castle doors heaved open as they approached. On the other side, Nicholas spotted a servant boy operating a winch. They were led into the wide entrance hall, where a man with a warrior's braid waited for them beneath the vaulted ceiling. He was impossible to overlook, massive and perfectly still among the busy servants crossing beneath the colonnade. There were twice as many insignia on his chest than any other guard.

"Malik Faisan."

Idris Ali, head of the king's shurta, had a voice like a beast. The hand he placed over his heart could have been a bear claw for how thick and heavy it sat. Malik copied the gesture and lowered his head, offering his ring in his palm. Ali took it and studied it closely.

Then, the first change: Malik bowed deep and pronounced, "A great shame has befallen my family. I come today to wipe away the ash my predecessors scattered over my good name."

He waited. "Proceed," said Ali.

"My grandmother and my father abandoned their lawful obligation to the crown. I cannot erase their disloyalty, but I will do my best to make amends. In accordance with the Law of Four, I offer my due service toward my country and my king."

"Stand."

Malik stood. "I request a formal audience with the king."

"That is not a simple request."

"I consider myself a high-priority guest."

Ali's thick beard ticked.

"I would like to meet the man I am swearing my life to. Is that unfair?"

Ali wore no expression, but he didn't appear to take Malik as a threat. He returned the ring. "I will bring your appeal to the chamberlain."

At the mention of Cairo, Nicholas' fingers itched to adjust his scarf. Only his eyes were visible, but he found himself angling his head downward anyway. Cairo carried a certain lurking feeling with him; Nicholas couldn't shake the sense that the advisor was watching them, leaning over the balcony of a higher floor with Nicholas' name on his tongue.

Ali cast a look at the servant with the winch. The boy piped up, "In the meantime, might our honored guest care for tea?"

Malik dipped his head once more. "Your hospitality is much appreciated."

The servant gestured with an arm. Malik, Adrian, and Nicholas started forward.

"The Faisan only."

They had expected this. It still made Nicholas' tongue feel fat.

"The king upholds stringent standards for his guests," Ali continued. "Only necessary visitors are allowed."

Now, the second change. Instead of sending Adrian a resolute smile and following alone, Malik squared his shoulders. "I am a cautious man, as any good Caldoran should be. Just as the king will surely have his men, I will have mine. Or do I not possess the right to a witness? If I did not know any better, I would deem these unfriendly terms."

The beard ticked again, enough this time that Nicholas could nearly see the mouth beneath it. Malik didn't waver even as he was loomed over, even as his words hung.

Finally, "Very well. You may bring one of your men."

Adrian's eyes went tight around the corners, but Malik seemed unbothered. They had prepared for this, too. Rather than feed any more tension, Malik acquiesced. Then he nodded to Nicholas.

They left Adrian behind with a lower ranking shurta and followed the servant boy. It was the first time Nicholas had walked the castle halls without a blindfold and in daylight, but he was walking into a dark spot in his vision. He had never written from Malik's perspective; all they knew of what came next was how it ended. Ali's hulking form cast shadows on them from behind. Despite the curiosity that nagged him to look his fill now that he had the chance, Nicholas kept his eyes low. He felt distinctly watched.

They waited in a lounging area of sorts, simple in its adornment, with a washstand and basin in one corner. Ali left them with another guard stationed outside the door. The servant excused himself and returned minutes later with steaming jasmine and savory cakes. They didn't speak. This was the part in the story where it all went wrong.

The door opened. Ali reentered. Nicholas did his best not to stiffen too visibly.

"The chamberlain has sanctioned your request and arranged for an audience at the earliest availability. You will see the king shortly."

He left, and that was all. No handcuffs, no accusations. No charges of desertion for breaking the Law of Four.

Nicholas downed his untouched tea in one gulp.

"If you would make your way to the washstand," said the servant. He scrubbed each of their hands vigorously with soap, water, and rough towelettes and gave no explanation. They had only just started toward the settee when Ali reappeared yet again.

He intercepted them in two steps. Malik was studying his raw, pink palms, so when Ali locked dark cuffs around his wrists, it looked almost as if he had offered them up.

14. Louder

Nicholas wished he could say he was surprised, but he had pretty much lived in worst case scenarios for the last two weeks. At least he was prepared for this one.

He lunged forward toward Malik before Ali could even state the cause for arrest. All he needed was one touch to unravel the magic-nullifying cero charm laced in the metal of the handcuffs. Apparently, his bad luck had yet to run out, because Nicholas did not get his one touch. The shurta who had been guarding the room a moment before yanked his arms behind him. A second set of shackles locked around his wrists.

Malik threw his weight. It should have been futile against the brick wall that was Ali, but Ali lurched like a young oak in a heavy wind, and Malik twisted away to face Nicholas. He threw his arms over Nicholas' shoulders and wiggled his hands beneath the scarf; at the first cool touch against Nicholas' neck, Malik transfigured the metal, and the cuffs clattered away.

Malik brought down the hanging lamp mounted above Nicholas' head, pulling Nicholas forward by the arm as the guard jumped back with a shout. Ali bouldered into their path as they ran to the door. Or, he would have, but the tile floor had folded over his feet. He overbalanced, toppling in place. It bought them enough time to make it out.

Malik touched the torch next to the door. Its glass bulb shuddered, jostling the flame within, as he said, "Morra."

As if the room inside had been plunged underwater, the shouting and footsteps went silent. The door did not open behind them.

The rest was a race against time. They unfortunately had to speed-walk it, as it was also a race against sound. They had little direction to guide them; only the awareness that they were on the castle's third floor, and a series of panels in the journal that showed Rayan on the fifth, fighting from a balcony that overshadowed the entrance hall. Malik studied those drawings intently as they hurried, only belatedly reaching back to free Nicholas' hands. He moved with the confidence of someone who had spent a lifetime relying on mental maps.

"What was that?" Nicholas asked on the stairs to the fourth floor. With every story, the halls seemed narrower and shorter, as if shrinking to a sharp peak.

"Dungeon charm." Malik was panting, face shiny with sweat. "It won't hold long. The talisman was shit." He held his hand to his face and muttered into his middle finger, "Sino. Adrian? Adrian, can you hear me?"

The Faisan ring, on the other hand, made a perfect talisman, even for a complicated bell charm that had been cast two hours before. Adrian's voice rang clear, a grave whisper of, What's wrong?

"I'm...under arrest," said Malik, so worn out he stumbled at the next staircase. Caught up in finding his way, he didn't seem to notice that he had flipped past those very words a few pages ago, where they were shown coming through the enchanted golden cuff wrapped around the shell of Adrian's ear.

Nicholas began to have a bad feeling.

"Don't do anything idioti-" Malik was saying when a crash sounded some-where far off. Shouting followed. "You idiot!"

He moved faster. They breached stairs to the topmost floor in time to see a figure in black burst from a room down the hall, closely followed by a warning yell from a female voice.

"Wait!" Malik called to the back of a dark-cherry head. Yasmin's stance was instantly defensive when she faced them. By the time her charge had followed suit, Nicholas and Malik had dropped to one knee and bowed their heads.

"Your Majesty," Malik spoke, probably out of turn, before there was time to act. "I believe you know who I am. Despite how it may seem-" he winced as more shouting sounded from below. "I haven't come to you seeking trouble. The direct opposite, I-"

"You," repeated the king, a question without the inflection.

"We. We seek a conversation. I swear on my family name, that is all, if you'll allow it."

"Raise your head." A moment later, "Both of you."

Nicholas complied and saw eyes focused on him. Look at me, they de-manded. Only a sliver could be seen of Nicholas' face, and he had been recognized by that sliver alone. They said so, clear as a reflection in stainless steel.

"The pecking viper strikes again," said Rayan, unamused. "Hello, Nico."

Then he said, "Yasmin," as he turned toward the balcony at the end of the hall.

Malik hurtled backward, bullied by an invisible force. As he went down coughing, Nicholas had the sense to throw off this coat. He felt it a second later - a buffet of air pummeling him backward, condensed and thrown by the tomite glowing indigo on Yasmin's right hand - but most of the blow dissipated the second it touched the skin of his arms, crossed over his chest.

Okay. He allowed a second to be impressed with himself as he started after Rayan. That's sick.

Yasmin came for him with a mad-dog snarl and was made to regret it when something slammed into her back. Malik wouldn't give up her attention so easily. Nicholas made his break for the balcony.

He could see everything from his vantage point. Adrian, surging up from the entrance hall in the direction Ali had led them away, skipping the stairs entirely to haul himself up on impossibly fat brambles as they wound around the banister lining the second floor. Swarming shurta, tripping as they ran after him as if the ground were shaking beneath them in tiny, concentrated earthquakes, throwing off their trajectory as they sent lance-head projectiles his way in waves. And the terrifying silhouette of the king leaning over the entrance hall, raising his hands then sweeping down.

The movement was violent and melodic. Spires of flame descended on Adrian. They narrowly missed as the prince climbed the wall like a lizard, wrapping the third-floor banister in thorns and vaulting upward.

Nicholas forced his voice over the noise. "Don't you understand?" Rayan didn't turn. He unwrapped his face, louder, louder. Across the entrance hall and a floor beneath them, Adrian heard him. "Try, please! I know you remember the book and I know you remember its strangeness, help us rewrite it- listen to me!"

He reached out. His hand landed half on Rayan's sleeve, half on his glove, and just barely glancing the skin between. The flames scattered into nothing. Nicholas thought again, sick-

"Do not touch me!"

It was vicious, so thick with disgust Nicholas thought he could hear the bile in Rayan's throat. He threw Nicholas to the floor. There was a moment in which Nicholas could hear only the pounding in his head. Then, past that, the prickly climb of branches right below them - Adrian had changed course. That was all buried by the sound of shattering glass.

Every torch in the entrance hall exploded. There was dimness for an instant, the only light coming purple-red through the windows. Rayan loomed, a phantom in his prime, arms raised like a conductor. Orange light exploded at the crescendo, so bright it took several blinks to clear his somber silhouette from Nicholas' vision. A figure took shape in the flames. Wide wings, a round head crowned with fanning, plumy wisps of fire. An arrowhead beak spread wide.

Nicholas' throat hurt from his short bout of shouting but he shouted again, some fraught plea as he pushed to his feet. An elbow locked around his neck before he could get far. At the very edges of his vision, Malik lay crumpled on the floor.

The fire roared like its own beast. Nicholas couldn't see with his chin forced upward, but knew how it looked, how easily the branches caught.

"Do you hear that?" Yasmin sneered at his throat. Somewhere, Adrian screamed. "You, next. I do not need vigalis to burn you, spy."

It was a terrible time to remember Dalisay's warning, the flames on her dais.

He put all of that honest fear onto his face, like he knew Yasmin wanted to see, as Malik opened up the floor behind her.

Malik called Adrian's name. Yasmin tossed Nicholas aside, but he grabbed her right back. His hold on her wrists only lasted a scarce couple of seconds against her strength. For those seconds, she had no magic. And in those seconds, fingerlike vines grasped at the edges of the hole in the floor.

"Saints almighty, you are on fire," Malik gasped as he hauled Adrian through.

"Put me out, then!"

They barreled through the closest door. It slammed in Yasmin's face. A yell rang through it, "Dungeo-!" then cut off as if dunked underwater.

Yasmin only wasted one failed push on the door before she grabbed Nicholas' wrist and slammed his hand to the wood. She charged in as glass sprayed across the office space and leaned over the smashed window, staring straight down five stories of castle wall and the rocky cliff above Lake Charlatan. A tall, narrow wave swelled up to wrap around Malik and Adrian's falling bodies like a glove, then pulled them under. The surface returned to stillness.

Nicholas was also leaning over the window, watching. So when Yasmin's rage shook the whole room, and the curtain rod crashed down on his upper back, he found himself following their lead. Except he didn't wear an ondate crystal to control the waves. He was not going to be gently snatched out of the air. He was going to splatter like a fly against a freeway windshield.

He understood, to an extent, how free fall worked. He was still shocked by how fast he dropped.

Though, he realized - maybe because he had the time to realize it - that he could have been falling faster. There was a feeling like punches against his back, bouncing him in the air. He imagined this was how it felt to fall through clouds in a cartoon. The pushback weakened the further he fell, and stopped altogether partway down the cliffside. But it had slowed his fall, so that when he hit the surface, he didn't paint it watercolor red.

He still touched down hard enough to feel his brain racket in his skull.

The world went silent. Plunged underwater.

His limbs wouldn't move. Must've hit his head hard. The water was too cold for swimming, anyway. He stopped trying and learned that he was weightless, and that he liked the feeling. He could move his eyelids, at least, so he looked. He was facing the sky. Salt stung his eyes. Lake Charlatan was not a lake at all, but a time-carved cove isolated from the sea. This water held so much history. Nicholas fell through time.

His vision darkened around the edges. The quiet was uncompromising. He could do anything, he could shout. Here, nobody would mind if he was loud. The water would suck up the sound; what a good listener! Nicholas opened his mouth and screamed as he lost consciousness.

□ □ □

He woke up vomiting. He coughed water and his dinner onto grass. Slowly, and after several tries, he opened salt-encrusted eyes and found that the world had become a blur. Somehow, through all of the fuzz, he still recognized the dark, dripping figure above him.

□ □ □

His body was cold, but making every effort to be warm. There was thin, dry clothing over his skin and a heavy blanket around his shoulders. More heat came from somewhere ahead, kissing his cheeks pink.

He extended his palms toward that warmth. That was when he felt the bindings around his wrist, and he remembered, and he understood.

"He's awake," a woman said behind him.

"I don't want to do this again," said Nicholas. "Can we not do this again?"

Footsteps circled to Nicholas' front. "You're a talented actor," said the king of Caldora.

"You're wasting your time."

"Fool me once, fool me twice." It was in his voice, too: look at me.

Nicholas didn't feel much like obeying, so he looked down at his lap. He remained like that as the questions started. It was all the same, if angrier this time around. Who, what, when, where, why are you? Nicholas didn't feel like answering, either.

Rayan's anger mounted fast. He leaned over Nicholas, demanding attention. "Speak, Viper, or-"

"Or what?" Nicholas said with his head low. "Will you hurt me, Your Majesty? Will you hit me? Aim for the head. Knock me the hell out so I don't have to do this again. Knock me so hard I forget all of it."

"Mind your tone," warned Yasmin, but Rayan's hand went up and she quieted.

"Mouthy today," he said. "Did your good sense drown in the lake? Or have you resolved to die for your stubbornness?"

"I won't die for anything," said Nicholas. "You won't kill me."

When he stood, he discovered that his ankle was bound to the chair. He wobbled off-balance. There was movement behind him, but Rayan raised his hand again.

"You've had every chance to kill me. You even had the chance today to let me die. But you saved me." When Nicholas finally looked up, Rayan's face was wide open. The fireplace at his back cast it all in brutal contrast. Fury in his eyes, fury in his lips, just as bright as Nicholas remembered. "You don't have it in you."

Rayan was searching. Looking for tells, but there was nothing to read. Nicholas had run out of feeling. As if playing catch-up, Rayan emptied his face in a hurry, racing to become expressionless.

"I've yet to hear a 'thank you,' by the way," he said.

"For what? Taking me hostage? My friends were in that water."

Something flew into Nicholas' chest, knocking him back onto the chair. His bag. It was open, so he could see his destroyed (and now waterlogged) laptop and phone inside, and all his soggy stationery. Nothing else. "Your friends took your book and left you for dead. I doubt you'd make a valuable hostage."

"You don't know as much as you think. They would've helped me."

"One wrong touch and the whole lot of you would have drowned." When Nicholas had no response for this, Rayan seemed satisfied (this was typical; to urge him to speak up, only to tire quickly of his voice). "You would do well not to overvalue yourself. You are only alive because you know something I don't. Since you have so much to say, why don't you introduce yourself? Honestly, this time."

"Hi there. I don't think we've met. You can call me...God, probably."

He was very aware that he was playing with fire. He was tired enough not to care. And anyway, Dalisay had told him to harden his skin.

"You are only alive because I dreamed you. I dreamed you and I wrote you down and now you've come off the page to make me miserable."

Rayan did not seem outraged or disbelieving or even put-off. Nicholas really must have left his good sense in the lake, because he observed this with disappointment.

"It is as Cairo speculated," Rayan murmured. Maybe he had already gone through all of the outrage and disbelief, had already doubted history and mourned his loss of agency. But his hair was still wet. He couldn't have had enough time to reckon with what it meant to be an imagination, to be two weeks old. Rayan met Yasmin's eye, nodded his head, and got back to business like that was all the comfort either of them needed. "How do we change it? That book of yours?"

"We, um," Nicholas stammered, thrown off by the quick turnaround. "You can't." On the journey from the frontier, they had tried everything. Erasing, overwriting, tearing, cutting, dousing, scratching. He told the king as much.

"So then you tried to defy it," Rayan gathered. "And that failed, too."

Nicholas couldn't be certain without the book in front of him, but when he recalled the pages in his head, it was obvious. None of the "changes" they'd planned out had been changes at all. They had added dialogue, maybe added a few steps between the panels, but when it came down to it, everything written had come to fruition. Nicholas nodded.

The fire behind Rayan flickered. It seemed anxious. He seemed anxious, though he masked it quickly.

"If you do not even know the rules yourself...who gave you the book?"

"A friend." Or so he'd thought. "A witch."

"It is decided, then. Yasmin."

With that, Rayan left the room. Yasmin crouched to free Nicholas' foot. For once, she wasn't glaring at him. Her gaze landed elsewhere. She was not so good at hiding her emotions.

There was no blindfold this time around. The message was clear: no point keeping him ignorant if they had no intention of releasing him. Nicholas looked around with little interest and didn't bother trying to learn the path.

Rayan walked several strides ahead. Yasmin shepherded Nicholas close at his back. They took him past cathedral doors into a space his wildest fantasies couldn't have conjured up. Saffron rugs and wooden columns and wall frescos, two stories of cloth-bound books on shelves that curved with the walls. At the center, a podium so high it required a set of stairs. There waited a brassy telescope beneath a skylight.

Nicholas saw his reflection in a dark window. His face was sunken and passive. He thought he looked more like himself than ever before.

In an hard-to-spot pocket between shelves, far from the room's open center, Rayan pulsed his fingers outward. The floor rippled open around them with a groan to reveal a staircase down. It was dark at the bottom until the torches sprang to life. More books, more shelves, though not nearly as loved. The room held in its circular walls a sense of shame. It was small and smelled of dust and earth.

"The only texts you will find in Caldora that so much as mention witchcraft are in this room," said Rayan. "They are strictly forbidden."

"I'm honored."

"You like to read, don't you?"

"You want me to look for a way to change the book."

"Surely you of all people understand the importance of wording. Try again."

"I...have to find a way."

"Read every last title if you must."

Nicholas glanced over the hundreds of spines.

"You can't exactly force me to read."

"I doubt I'll have to." The torches kicked up a notch, shedding enough light for reading. "Every piece you learn about your accursed journal will bring you a step closer to...wherever you're from." He waved a dismissive hand and sent a random book Nicholas' way. "And, besides. You don't have it in you, either."

Nicholas was soon alone, clutching a dusty leather volume on illegal charms and seeing the king long after the ceiling had closed up behind him. In particular, Nicholas saw him in the journal's final pages, bleeding down the stalk that impaled his chest. Rayan was going to die. And if the logic was twisted just so, into something deformed and accusatory, Nicholas was the one killing him.

15. Rhythm

The forbidden archive, as Nicholas came to call it, was not nearly as exciting as the nickname suggested. He had tried it out in several voices in the hopes that a sense of drama would make this all more bearable, then registered that he hadn't been down here long enough to start talking to himself and stopped mid-whisper.

He thought it was his third day. He couldn't be sure.

The torches never went out; he went to sleep and woke up in the same orange light. There was no way to measure time. The best he could do was to pass it. And the only way to pass it was to read.

He supposed that was what Rayan wanted.

There was a large stack of books near the sofa. He had spent his first day painstakingly scouring half of the shelves, picking out anything that mentioned witchcraft within the first page. The rest of his time had been devoted to moving through the pile itself, struggling with faded script, curly handwriting, and the sort of language he had hated reading in his old literature classes. He would never finish if he went word-for-word, but he couldn't afford to skim too light and miss anything, either, and towing that balance had left him with a permanent headache.

So far, he had learned the names and life stories of several autobiographical and heavily poetic witches, how to hide his budding magical abilities, so many potion recipes, recipes that didn't seem to have anything to to with witchcraft at all, the geographical distribution of kova zem, the date and method of many Maesian executions...

He had gathered in bits and pieces that there were more zem than the nine he had invented, and that the control of these alternative stones constituted "witchcraft." But any mention of them was closely followed by words scratched off the paper, or paragraphs covered by ink spills, or even entire pages torn from the binding.

Nicholas was losing what little hope he'd had to begin with. He kept his water-wrinkled pad of sticky notes at his side to mark pages that might be even remotely helpful and hadn't used a single one. His pile of discarded books was growing, and yet the original pile hardly seemed to have shrunk at all. He wasn't any closer to unearthing how he had gotten here or how to leave. And he wasn't any closer to saving Rayan.

He wasn't sure how much he wanted to. The fact that he was contemplating his own morality over a storybook villain irritated him to no end. But if the events in the journal really were set in stone, Rayan would die by Nicholas' pen. No matter how awful he was, that didn't feel right, not now that he had become flesh and bone and breath. Maybe it was because of how awful he was- or, how awful he wasn't. Unkind, warmongering, temperamental, sure. Absolutely the cause of most of Nicholas' problems. But bad enough to die?

Nicholas wasn't sure Rayan had done enough to deserve that. Either way, he didn't like being the one to decide.

The only place to sleep was the sofa, tucked into a reading nook across from the stairs. It was long enough if he bent his knees. There was an armchair, too, but he only moved to it when he felt himself fossilizing in place. Three times a day, he was fed like a hungry circus lion in a cage. The ceiling opened up, a guard floated a tray of food down onto the stairs, the ceiling closed again. Those were the only glimpses of daylight he got.

He had a lot to be pissed about, but that particular hit tipped him over the edge.

On that third day, he did his reading from the stairs, as high up as he could sit without bending his neck against the ceiling. The shurta who appeared holding his dinner didn't outwardly flinch, but there were instantly four conical blades hovering threateningly above the hole in the ceiling. The ceiling where Nicholas had laid his hand so that it couldn't be magically closed.

"I'm not gonna leave," he said dryly. "I'm not dumb."

"Could have fooled me," said the guard. "If you're so smart, you'll distance yourself from the exit."

Nicholas had no interest in bantering with a man who had sharp objects pointed at his neck, so he cut to the chase. "I want a window."

"I said-"

"I heard you. I said I want a window. How am I supposed to work when my circadian rhythm is all confused?"

The guard narrowed his eyes. "Cicadoran rhyth-? You're underground!" His voice slipped into exasperation before he caught himself and squared his shoulders. "A window is impossible. Withdraw. I will not ask again."

"Do you even have clearance to harm me? Boss might get pretty mad if something gets in the way of my very important work. Where's your diplomacy? I'm not asking a lot. But if it's too much for you, take it up with the big man. Or bring Rayan down here and let me talk to him myself."

"You impudent-"

"Anyway. I'll get to work now. Very slowly, until I have my window."

He emerged just far enough to take the tray out of the guard's hands and went down the staircase. His own hands were shaking, but here in his dungeon, he was the only witness. He ate at the base of the stairs and comforted himself by picturing how Malik and Adrian would react to his behavior. Malik would be horrified, irritated, and secretly a bit impressed. Adrian would laugh big and loud and throw an arm over Nicholas' shoulder. Where have you been hiding all that?

I don't know, thought Nicholas. I don't know where it came from and I don't think I like it.

He was still on the floor, twisted at an odd angle so the torchlight didn't cast shadows over Bedtime Stories for the Little Witch, when the room shook. Shapeless voices drifted down from the library above and didn't stop for several minutes. There was a lot of rumbling, a lot of creaking, then nothing again, except for the gentle groan of the ceiling opening up the way it did at mealtimes. But he'd had all of his meals already. And the ceiling didn't close again.

Nicholas gave the ceiling a good minute to decide it was sure. Then he went to check it out. Upstairs was a window.

It was taller than him, a round-topped pane in the library wall that overlooked Lake Charlatan far below. He rapped his knuckles against the glass; it was thick. Not that he had any desire to dive to his death again. He didn't remember seeing it when he'd come through the library days ago. The rest was definitely new.

Three doorless walls enclosed the top of the staircase and a bed situated beneath the window. There was space to take maybe four steps in any direction. Small steps.

Nicholas grinned.

He knelt on the bed. The sheets were thin, but the mattress had a nice give, and Caldoran summer nights were sweaty, anyway. Through the window, he could see the stars. He could see the moon. Once in the sky, once in the lake's reflection.

Nicholas turned around with plans to fall blissfully back into the sheets like he'd seen in movies and nearly jumped off the bed instead.

"Oh, what the hell."

Rayan looked at Nicholas like somehow he was the crazy one.

"You have your window," he said, leaning against the opposite wall. "But allow me to be very clear: you will not get along here by throwing tantrums to have your way. You are not a guest. You are going to behave, do you understand?"

"I want a clock, too," said Nicholas.

"You were smarter before."

"You said you wouldn't punish me for speaking my mind."

"The situation was different."

"Is there anything else you need, or..."

Rayan looked for a second like he didn't understand the question. Nicholas saw the moment it clicked and recognized that he might have pushed too far.

"Are you trying to dismiss me?"

There was no inflection in his voice, just a cold steel grind. Nicholas' throat did its best to crawl into itself. It was a familiar feeling. It was how he'd always reacted in the face of authority or power. Unobtrusive and non-confrontational. Dull but likable. Inoffensive, unremarkable, harmless, trustworthy, unheard.

He forced his voice forward. "Should I be more direct?"

Rayan's long legs brought him before the bed in two strides. "I own everything within these walls."

Nicholas refused to crane his head the way he knew Rayan wanted. Instead, he stood and walked to the stairs, offering a slight bow as he passed. "Not everything," he said. "Have fun lurking. I've got work to do."

Footsteps followed him down. Nicholas cursed whatever saints Rayan worshiped. He tried to act as though he didn't notice, grabbing a new book from the pile just so he didn't have to turn around. But Rayan's presence loomed heavy behind him, and when the king reached over him for a book, Nicholas shuddered to his fingertips and snapped, "What are you doing?"

Rayan's fingers paused over a time-stained leather cover.

"Turn around," he said. Nicholas obeyed before he could think, tugged by the quiet danger in Rayan's tone. "Listen carefully. You are standing on my floor holding my book. You will sleep on my bed beneath my window. You live off of my food and water, and my generosity. Every step you take within these walls - every step you take on this soil - it all belongs to me. I will not be questioned for treading over my own earth, and you will not act as though I owe you any explanation. Say you understand."

"I understand."

Rayan took the sofa. Nicholas sank onto the armchair like a stone dropped in still water, rigid and out of place. But Rayan didn't acknowledge him again, and the goosebumps faded and his stomach settled, and they read through the night.

The next morning, his breakfast was delivered through a slit in the upstairs wall. With it was a small analog clock. Nicholas propped it on the windowsill, but he eventually had to turn it around. He was glancing at it often, disheartened every time by how little it moved. Not that he had anything to look forward to.

At least he could read under the light of the sun.

It made him think of Adrian again. He had been trying not to do that too much.

Where were he and Malik right then? Were they okay? Were they worried about Nicholas? Were they...

He laid his book on witchy pet care over his face. It smelled of must.

Malik cared for Adrian. That was clear as day to Nicholas, maybe because Malik was so much like himself. But Adrian...he had liked Nicholas, hadn't he? Or was Nicholas so starved for attention, he had misconstrued all of the touching and the smiling and-

It didn't matter. Adrian and Malik had been written for each other. They were inevitable.

Malik was the fictional projection of a prettier, more interesting version of himself. Adrian was the fictional projection of the boy of his dreams. Nicholas felt gross.

He missed having company. He missed the noise of it all.

He was so lonely, he might have even appreciated it when someone barged into his peace and quiet two nights later, if that someone had been anybody else. Rayan didn't say a word as he came downstairs. Nicholas stiffened as he approached, kicking his legs off the armrest, but Rayan only took another book from the pile and settled into the armchair.

It became an irregular pattern. Rayan would appear without preamble or greeting, always at night. There were no torches upstairs, so they read in the forbidden archive together, though "together" was a generous word. Even in the same room, the king occupied his own space.

It was annoying, but Nicholas guessed that if his life was on the line, he'd have trouble leaving his survival in someone else's hand, too. Two sets of eyes were faster than one, though Rayan made it hard to focus. Nicholas read slower when he was around. He thought better of telling him that.

The first time Rayan broke the silence, it was to tell Nicholas, "You're falling asleep."

Nicholas straightened from his slouch. He had made the mistake once of drifting off on the armchair over a book on potion chemistry. He'd woken up with his head lolled back as if he'd died there, and with such an excruciating pain in his neck he almost wished he had.

"I'm fine," he said, blinking the haze from his eyes to look down at his book on...potion history.

"There's drool on your chin."

Nicholas wiped his face with his sleeve. Very thoroughly, so Rayan wouldn't see his flaring cheeks. Rayan coughed into his fist.

"'S your fault for destroying my sleep schedule," Nicholas grumbled. And just when he'd started getting his circadian rhythm in order.

"My job is not to idle on a throne, you know. I have business to attend to during the day. I never asked that you stay up. Go to bed."

"I'm not falling asleep in the same room as the evil king, thanks."

"And how are you so sure that I'm evil?" said Rayan. "I studied that page well. The one where you described me as surly, distant, detached, severe, domineering, short-tempered, haughty - the list goes on."

"What are you getting at?"

"You called me cold, but not cold-hearted. Nowhere does it say I am to be evil. Or wicked, or malicious, or vindictive, or anything of the sort."

"That won't work," said Nicholas. "I know you."

"Do you." Rayan thought a second. Nicholas could see it in the tap of his fingers against his open book. "What time of day do I like the least?"

"Is this what you think it means to know someone?"

"Isn't it?"

Nicholas realized he wasn't too familiar with the whole thing himself.

"Ok. I don't know you. But does anyone?"

Rayan rolled his shoulders. Stumped.

"People might have, once. Or..." his gaze drifted, and he began to mumble. "I suppose they never did, if my existence only began when you wrote it. I don't know what to make of it, that history is fake and all of my memories are meaningless."

Nicholas said, "I don't care."

"Of course."

They returned to their work.

Sometime later, Rayan perked up in his seat. "Listen to this," he said, and read aloud, "Wherever reality exists, so exists the ability to alter it. This is the foundation of what we call witchcraft or sorcery, though it may take on a different name elsewhere."

Nicholas had been nodding off again, but that woke him up. He was in front of the couch in a second, bending awkwardly forward to read.

"What else does it say?" he asked. Because the words were upside-down.

"Nothing of note," said Rayan, angling the page toward himself with a wary glance at Nicholas. "But this suggests..."

"The existence of 'elsewhere.' Another world, or- many worlds."

"All with something in common." He looked up urgently. "Yours, tell me about it. Your world. Tell me about the magic."

"There was none."

"Clearly there was."

"I don't know! It was- hidden, I guess, or...I don't know."

"Do you mean to say you invented all of..." He made a vague, all-encompassing gesture. "This? Based on nothing?"

His tone made Nicholas bristle. "That's the point of fantasy."

"That is absurd."

"Excuse me?"

"Running off into some unreal world in your head like a child." Rayan chuckled in a way that was very intentionally fake. "Why would you waste your time that way?"

Nicholas hated this question. He'd heard it all through his undergrad, that he was throwing away his talent, that he was selling out before he'd even gotten started. He had nodded his head and bitten his tongue until it bled, saturated in shame.

"I wanted to be anywhere but where I was," he said, bleak and unyielding. "It kept me sane."

"From where I'm sitting, it certainly looks like insanity."

"You sit on a throne," Nicholas snapped. "Your real world has always served you."

He was forced back a step when Rayan stood.

"You really don't know me." He dropped the book between them, forcing Nicholas to fumble to catch it, and stepped around him. "In any case, there is no 'always.' Always was only in my head, apparently."

Nicholas watched him leave. When Rayan took his last step onto the higher floor, and he couldn't see Nicholas and Nicholas couldn't see him, Nicholas said, "I don't think your memories are meaningless."

He didn't call out, but his voice carried in the silent underground. He heard when Rayan's footsteps paused. "This land was shaped by its history; you were shaped by yours. Those things are undeniable. If your memories have a taste and a smell and a feeling, that has to mean something. It means you lived them. Even if it happened in the blink of an eye, or- I don't understand it. I don't think I can. But I've given up on logic at this point."

The king left him to his reading.

◻ ◻ ◻

Nicholas came to observe that Rayan had many shades. They were subtle, and gray, and easier to tell apart with time. Most nights, he was iron. Straight-shouldered and clean-pressed. Measured, magnetic, commanding attention without saying anything. But there were some nights, the ones that really kept Nicholas up late, when the king arrived after midnight with his coat rumpled like he had thrown it on in a haste. His hair seemed like an afterthought, messily tied back and pillow-frizzed, and his gloved fingers were restless against the pages. He was quiet in both states, but his silence was louder in this heather gray. Either way, he was distracting. Nicholas wished he would leave.

It was a dark heather night. Rayan's vest was buttoned unevenly. Nicholas had gotten used to napping during the day to adjust to the king's inconsiderate timing, but it still felt like being ripped from sleep when he heard a book thud against the floor and looked up to see Rayan on his feet.

"Tell me, Viper," he said, for once hiding nothing. Nicholas couldn't believe how young he looked when he admitted with his face how he felt. Right then, he felt afraid. "What possessed you to write this?"

"...Huh?"

"Is this your idea of a happy ending? Does everyone cheer when the villain dies? It's cruel, isn't it?"

He didn't stick around for an answer. The torch flames bounced angrily in their bulbs. They didn't settle until Rayan was gone.

16. Eye to Eye

"M ust you?"

Rayan's voice normally brought Nicholas an irritation that settled heavy over his bones, but tonight, he was more than happy to lower his
book until he could see the king over the edge. It was a seemingly endless
anthology, and an even bigger headache than Rayan; who knew witches
were so flowery?

"What?"

"Must you do that," said Rayan from the sofa, which he seemed to have
claimed as his own. "Constantly."

"What are you talking about."

Rayan narrowed his eyes. "You're buzzing. You're a bee."

"Right, that helps."

Rayan hummed a single note to a very flat tune. "Every night. For hours.
It's driving me mad."

Nicholas raised his book again as his cheeks grew hot. He hadn't realized he'd been humming. How long had Rayan held his tongue? It couldn't have been the entire time. Those first few nights, Nicholas had been so keyed up over the king's presence he was aware of his own breathing, let alone any noise he made. But he had been in the archive seventeen nights now, give or take a few, and he'd seen Rayan on most of them.

Comfort was a quiet, slippery thing, and a mistake he couldn't afford. He would have to watch himself.

"I normally listen to music when I read," he said. "I guess I...yeah."

"Why would you do that?"

"It helps me focus."

"...If I brought a band down here, you would read faster?"

"That would be extremely distracting."

"Well something has to change!" Rayan was on his feet. Nicholas hid behind the anthology, using it to block out Rayan's stony face and sulking lower in his seat. "We aren't getting anywhere."

"I'm trying."

"Are you? Or are you biding your time until mine runs out? It is running out, isn't it?"

Nicholas didn't acknowledge the dig at his character except to inch the book downward so Rayan could see how much it annoyed him. "I don't know. There's no timeline in the journal."

Rayan muttered a curse. "It could be tomorrow."

"It won't be tomorrow."

"That isn't the point!" He began to pace, though with his legs and the small space, it looked closer to turning around in place. "You need to do better. You need to be better. That ending has to go, all of it."

He was watching Nicholas' face, so Nicholas kept it as blank as possible. It didn't work. The pacing stopped.

"You do understand you are expected to change all of it?"

If he could figure out how, Nicholas was going to save Rayan's life. He had decided on that right away. But the hero would win, just as he was supposed to. Nicholas wasn't about to betray the only friend he had in this world. In any world, maybe.

"Don't go back to faking mute now." Rayan stepped up to the armchair. Nicholas looked down at his book. "You can't have honestly thought I would let you off with a partial fix."

"You aren't letting me off at all."

"How are you so intent on protecting a stranger? You knew him a week."

"I've known him for years."

"I don't give a damn about the man you thought you knew in those delusional years you spent in your head, I am asking about the boy you met. What-"

"Jesus Christ-" the book tumbled to the floor- "If you ask me about his favorite goddamn time of day-"

"Je- who?"

"A week is plenty of time when the person you're learning wants to be learned. People are observable. You would know that if you ever paid attention to anyone but yourself."

Rayan bent forward, leering over the armchair with his hands clasped behind him. "And what have you observed? What did you learn from your prince's behavior that makes him so deserving of a hero's end?"

Nicholas was tired of this game. Of being analyzed and condescended to, questioned and questioned again as if Rayan knew any better than he did, towered over like some playground power trip. So he stood up, and he stepped forward, and instead of raising his chin he glared from beneath his lashes. "Is this really how you want to spend your time? Your clock is ticking, remember?"

Rayan didn't take the bait, or react at all. Nicholas was watching for it, itching for it, but Rayan wasn't even looking him in the eye, which was about the most irritating way he could react. Instead, he stared down the space between them. Nicholas tasted acid on the tip of his tongue, but before he could spit it all over Rayan's stupid fucking pasty face-

His eyes finally flicked to Nicholas'. "Back up."

Nicholas didn't exactly have much room. He had half a mind to tell Rayan to swallow his ego and back up himself if he needed his space so badly. But he had enough wits about him to move until his legs hit the chair.

"He beckons people closer," said Nicholas. "Adrian. He puts kindness before trust. He's...loud, and in your face. But he meets you where you are instead of demanding or prying or- he doesn't let anyone feel lonely, no matter how hard they try. He's blue-blooded and it shows, but he tries to be humble. He's ambitious and...self-deprecating. He puts everything on his own shoulders because he cares so much."

Rayan's jaw shifted. "And what have you observed in me?"

It sounded like a trap, but there was an unusual roundness to his eyes.

"Arrogance. Disdain. Emotional constipation on, like, a clinical level. You handle other people like a game, but they'd better not try to play on their own terms. You enjoy throwing your position around and you treat your best friends like your subordinates. No one can get too close. You're self-absorbed, invasive, cagey, insecure, condescending, and absolutely ter-rified of dying."

Rayan raised his eyebrows. "I've made quite the impression."

"Fitting for a king."

"You're naive if you don't see the bias in your own perception."

"Because it reflects how I've been treated? What do you think perception is?"

"You don't realize how ungrateful you are. Have you once considered how I could be treating you after all the trouble you've caused?"

Nicholas bowed as far as he could without touching his head to the king's chest. "Thank you, Your Majesty, for imprisoning me. Twice."

"Is this what you call prison?" Rayan raised his arms to the room around him, voice high on a laugh. "The first thing I ever did was release you from prison, or have you forgotten?"

"You mean so you could scrutinize me from the comfort of your own home? Real generous."

Rayan started to argue, but Nicholas raised a hand.

"Shut up," said Nicholas.

"Excuse-?"

"Shut the fuck up, oh my God, I'm an idiot."

"How dare- well, yes."

"The jail." Nicholas brought his hands to his head. He could rip his own hair out. "When I crashed down in North Simona."

Rayan nodded the way adults nodded to babbling toddlers. "Yes. There was a jail."

"Shut up, shut up!"

"Some kings would have you flogged for that mouth of yours."

Nicholas dropped back onto the armchair, bouncing slightly on the cushion. "Across from my cell! There was- the lady-"

"Yes, of course, I know the lady."

"I'm gonna kill you."

Rayan's mouth twitched. "Fairly certain that's grounds for beheading."

"She was a witch!"

He had nothing smart to say to that.

"She was arrested for witchcraft. A love potion that worked too well."

"She must have been transferred to Pondtam by now." Rayan was already in motion, pacing another short moment before starting for the stairs. "I'll have a driver ready for you in the morning. I will send a scribe along- or perhaps an investigator- I must look into Cairo's affairs-"

Nicholas blanched. "Cairo?" He didn't trust the chamberlain alone in a small space. "You mean you aren't going yourself?"

Rayan paused on the second step. "And why would I do that?"

"This is life and death you're talking about, and you're leaving it up to someone else? Is that what it means to be a king, sending others off to do your bidding so you never have to step foot out of your-"

"You really," Rayan said, turning over his shoulder with a cold stare that Nicholas felt to the soles of his feet, "need to learn to hold your tongue on matters you don't understand."

Nicholas didn't know why he kept pushing. God knows his life would be easier if Rayan stayed behind. There was no explaining it, the hotness in his gut. The urge to challenge, to provoke, to piss off a man who could wipe him off the face of this world and every other with the sweep of his hand.

It was unlike himself. But it didn't feel that way when he leaned forward in his seat and said, "Coward."

□ □ □

By "in the morning," Rayan had apparently meant the ass-crack of dawn. A driver was ready and waiting outside of the entrance hall as promised. He commanded four black horses. A shurta in all gray sat atop one; he and his horse were unblinking. The coach was small. A try at discretion, maybe, but the midnight walls and silver leaf gilding weren't exactly subtle. Nicholas was pushed down onto the single row of blue velvet seats. A table took up most of the floor space. It was honestly nice. He should probably be concerned about how cozy he had gotten with having his wrists cuffed.

A whispered argument floated through the window in the far door.

"You will take the center seat."

"I will not."

Nicholas tipped forward to see out the back of the window. Yasmin looked about ready to throw Rayan into the car. Nicholas hadn't thought he would actually come.

"As your guard, it is my duty-"

"I do not care. Sit."

"This is unbelievably petty."

"Come again? Was that, 'Yes, Your Majesty'?"

He seemed lively. Nicholas wasn't sure he could deal with that after three hours of sleep.

"You're behaving like a child."

"You're behaving like a woman who wants to lose her job."

It was such an empty threat, Yasmin didn't even humor it. She clenched her fingers in front of his neck and screamed soundlessly. It looked like she needed it. Then yanked the door open, blank-faced, and knelt to help Rayan inside. She took the middle, glaring at Nicholas for no reason as she sat. Rayan didn't look his way at all.

The driver kept to secluded woodsy roads. The quiet between Yasmin and Rayan felt unnatural. Nicholas didn't have any basis for that except the heaviness in the air. He wondered, between the two of them, who was the talker when they were alone. He couldn't imagine it was Rayan. Maybe Yasmin was a different person outside of work. Or maybe it was Cairo. The three of them.

It had taken something like an hour to pass Pondtam Prison the last time. He could handle one uncomfortable hour. Probably fifty minutes, now.

His leg started jittering somewhere around the thirty minute mark. Yasmin's eyes cut swiftly sideways and he used his bound hands to press his leg still.

The horses screeched. The car shuddered.

Yasmin was on alert immediately. Hooves thundered against the ground, pitching the coach forward before stopping it in place. An arm plunged through the window to Rayan's left and latched onto his hand. The force of the pull bunched Rayan's glove up to his knuckles. That was as far as it got before Yasmin grabbed the assailant by the meat of their thumb. There was an awful crunch and a scream, and the hand went limp. Rayan's glove and rings fell to the coach floor.

"This is why I sit by the door," Yasmin grumbled as she launched herself over Rayan's lap and out of the coach. Through either door, Nicholas could see several dark figures emerging from the woods. Shurta gray joined the picture as the guard, the driver, and Yasmin dove in to fight. They were outnumbered, and not just by the figures in black. The horses whined and stomped as hulking beasts with leathery gray skin closed in on the coach.

Nicholas knew them down to the peach-fuzz hair covering their backs. He had decided on the curled tails, the disklike faces, the sagging eyelids that made the Wahkong look like they had no eyes at all. But nothing could have prepared him for the piercing shriek that came from one beast's wide, flat-toothed mouth just before it charged at his door.

The coach toppled. Nicholas was thrown onto the table with a feeling like his spine buckling. Another heavy impact forced the seats off the wall. Wood splintered. Nicholas crashed.

His ears were ringing. Through the static, he heard the clamor of a fight. He craned over his shoulder to look past the wreckage of the seats on top of him, and saw two huge flat feet coming down like a mallet on the door he had sat against seconds before. Some force threw the beast sideways before the strike could land.

Then he looked down and saw Rayan's face, sheet-white beneath him. His eyes were foggy. He was staring up, not through the window but at his own bare hand. Where the attacker had touched him.

"Hey," said Nicholas. He tried to squirm off of Rayan and found himself stuck. "Hey, shouldn't you..."

He trailed off. Rayan wasn't hearing him.

"Hey. Earth to His Majesty." He imagined what would happen if those mallet-feet made it through the door. One good stomp could grind them into dust. "Your Majesty. Sir. Rayan."

Rayan's gaze flickered to his, but Nicholas may as well have been translucent.

"Oh, for fuck's sake." A glint of metal near Rayan's head caught Nicholas' eye, nearly hidden by the dark hair that had come undone around the king's face. Nicholas wriggled his hands out from the tight press of their chests. Rayan flinched with his whole body; Nicholas could feel it everywhere. "I'm not gonna touch you! Just..." He collected all five of Rayan's rings. "Put these on."

The rise and fall of Rayan's chest, and the heartbeat behind it, pushed erratically against Nicholas' ribs.

"Hey!" Nicholas urged. "Wake up. Now is not the time to have a meltdown. We're stuck. We're stuck in a tiny wooden box and there are men with monsters trying to break us in half. You need to do something."

Rayan looked like he was going to puke. If it came to that, Nicholas might prefer to let the Wahkong take them.

"I..." said Rayan. "I don't..."

"'I don't' my ass! Like hell you don't!" Nicholas didn't know what he was talking about. It couldn't have mattered nearly as much as the beasts knocking on their door. "I don't give a damn about your hysteria, you selfish fuck. Wake. Up. You can freak over a little skin-to-skin later, or internalize it with some unhealthy coping mechanism, or- shit, whatever, here!"

Nicholas held up the missing glove. Rayan jerked to grab for it, then hissed in pain. His right arm was caught beneath the fallen table.

"Shit. Okay."

"Don't," said Rayan when Nicholas reached for his hands.

"Trust me!" If his life wasn't on the line, Nicholas would have laughed at how ridiculous that was. With a level of care they really didn't have time for, he held the thumb of the glove with one hand and the pinkie with the other and spread them. He angled his palms as far away as the cuffs allowed. Plenty of room if Rayan moved slowly.

And he did. Painfully so. But he moved nonetheless, pushing his fingers through.

Nicholas slid each ring into place - tomite, encaline, vigalis, forcate, inercium. Pinkie to thumb. Rayan didn't move right away. A harsh pound above them sent the door slamming inward off its hinges.

"I am not going to die because of some deep-seated trauma that was never a part of your character to begin with. Wake the fuck up."

Nicholas could have cried in relief when Rayan glared up at him. The king let his head fall back and spat, "Fuck you."

He lifted the table enough to snake his arm free. Then he bracketed his arms around Nicholas, pressing his hands to the seats crushing them together. The weight eased from Nicholas' back. The busted seat went straight through the open door, leaving a gaping hole where the frame was, and the Wahkong grunted as it was forced back.

Rayan shoved Nicholas off. "Stay here," he said as Nicholas flopped onto his back like a grounded fish. Rayan jumped up, grabbed onto the jagged wood, and pulled himself into the fray.

Orange burst beyond the gap. Nicholas felt the heat of it. He heard Rayan's voice and locked onto it with all of his focus to drown out the sound of screaming.

"You hardly needed me."

The noise that followed was so foreign, it took Nicholas several seconds to process it as Yasmin's laughter.

"Useless king."

Nicholas lay there watching smoke puff into the sky as the commotion faded to nothing.

The carriage was righted without warning. He caught himself on his hands and knees on the floor. Then he stood on wobbling legs and emerged through the hole where the door had been.

One of the Wahkong lay dying on the road. The rest must have fled into the trees. As for the attackers, well- Nicholas didn't have starting numbers, but he didn't think there were any survivors. He counted thirteen bodies. Most bled from open wounds. Some still had lance-head blades sticking from their chests. A couple had been burnt beyond recognition.

"I told you to stay inside," said Rayan. Standing at the center of the disaster, panting and disheveled but otherwise unharmed, he looked every part the brutal villain. Powerful, fearsome, striking as a car crash- or a firework. Untouchable, if not for the clammy gray sheen to his skin. He kept a stubbornness to his stance, like he had something to prove now. Doubt my strength, I dare you.

Nicholas would never.

Yasmin knelt before the heaving beast. "Peace to your soul," she muttered before she slit its throat.

"Who were those people?" Nicholas heard his voice from somewhere outside of himself.

"You don't listen," said Rayan. "You don't fucking listen."

"Zemi Bandits. They steal kova zem for the handsome price," said Yasmin.

Nicholas staggered toward the tree line. "I told you," Rayan called after him, voice ragged. "I told you to stay-"

Nicholas dropped to his knees in the dirt and vomited.

17. Crescendo

A new coach arrived for them within the hour.

The horses were shaken and roughed up but uninjured. The driver took the calmest of the four and raced for the castle. Yasmin tried to convince Rayan to go home, try again another day; Rayan shut her down with cold decisiveness. Nicholas heard all of this from a distance, with his back turned. As far as he could get from the wreckage before Yasmin barked at him to stop.

Rayan crouched next to him. Behind them, the others were dealing with the disaster. With the corpses. Nicholas shuddered.

"Your hands," said Rayan. Nicholas saw that he was holding a key. Rayan freed Nicholas' hands, then returned his own to his lap. His right hand scratched at the palm of his left, digging into the fabric of the glove as if trying to scrape away something underneath. "Only until you pull yourself together."

He noticed Nicholas watching his hands and folded them. Nicholas wrapped his arms around himself.

"Would you have rathered we let them take our stones? Those groups don't leave witnesses."

"I didn't say anything," said Nicholas.

"It's bigger than self defense. It's the defense of the kingdom. If such acts against the crown were taken lightly, there wouldn't be a crown for much longer."

"I understand."

"It isn't as if I enjoy-" Rayan paused. His lips pressed together. Confused. "I don't have to explain myself to you."

"I never asked you to."

Nicholas watched him start to speak, then decide against it. Rayan turned his head away. They waited there a long while.

The second coach was black down to the spokes. Otherwise, the road was bare, like the fight had never happened. It took some time to hook up the old horses - there were six in total now, and four shurta. Nicholas spent that time counting his breaths so he wouldn't hurl the second they started moving and make himself Yasmin's next victim. Rayan still looked sick. He took the middle seat without complaint. Nicholas could see on Yasmin's face that she wanted to protest again, but the air around Rayan left no room for discussion. Nicholas was back in his cuffs.

They arrived in thirty minutes. Pondtam Prison was a strict rectangular building with vast stone walls. There was little to discern from the outside, just a sense of finality that reminded Nicholas of nearly drowning. Only the gatehouse guarding the front wall gave it any sense of time or feeling. That is, centuries old and baleful.

The driver strode to the iron grate and spoke to one of the shurta posted there. The grate was lifted with haste, and the prison guard vanished into the dark. He came back with two other men. Only then did Yasmin emerge from the coach and help Rayan down. She let the door close behind them, so Nicholas had to shoulder his way out. His momentum nearly landed him on his ass in the road, but at least no one saw him stumble. Everyone facing them had dropped onto one knee.

"Rise. I would like to do this as quickly as possible."

The last to obey was a young man, maybe a boy, swimming in his coat. He glanced up hesitantly, like he thought it might be illegal to stand in the presence of the king, before jumping to his feet so fast he looked dizzy afterward. The oldest of them, a man in a frock coat and a cap, spoke for the group.

"What a pleasant surprise, Your Majesty. May I introduce-"

"Did you hear me, warden?"

The warden took it in stride. He was tall, and might have once looked strong and frightening. Now, he mostly looked frightening. "Very efficient, Your Majesty. Did you hear him, boy?"

The young man darted ahead, whipped back around, bowed so deep he nearly kissed his knees, then continued to the other side of the grate to close it after them. Rayan and the warden headed the group, with Yasmin right behind them, and Nicholas behind her. One of Rayan's guards walked close at his side. Apparently, he got a real kick out of shepherding a prisoner. He kept shouldering Nicholas into place as if they weren't walking down a straight path.

Past the gatehouse was the entrance to the prison itself. It was a short walk. Nicholas tripped six times over the course of it. Rayan was in the middle of his discussion with the warden when he turned over his shoulder with narrowed eyes and said, "You're irritating me." But he was looking at the guard.

The pushing stopped. They bypassed a grim reception room with too few benches for the space or the visitors. A woman hovered at the desk, trying for the attention of a clerk who behaved as if the bars separating them blocked sound. The young man held open a door to a barren conference room and pulled out chairs for the warden and the king.

"Sit," said Rayan. Nicholas awkwardly kicked one out for himself. His guard's shadow fell over him from behind.

"Offer the guests a drink, boy."

"Right! Would-"

"No, thank you," Yasmin said as Rayan wrinkled his nose. So the boy stood at the door, sweating through his uniform.

"This prisoner you're looking for," said the warden. "The witch. What can you tell me about her?"

Rayan looked to Nicholas. Nicholas hadn't realized he was going to have to speak.

"Oh. Um. She was probably arrested four weeks ago? Or five. Long brown hair, super thin, kind of rambly...It was something about a love potion. A woman asked for it, but it worked too well, so she reported it to the graymen."

His chair rattled as the guard kicked one leg. Grayman was a colloquial term. Nicholas hadn't written it to be an insult, but apparently shurta took it that way.

"Is that all you remember?" asked the warden.

"There was also a rat."

"A...rat?"

"An albino rat."

There was something edgy in the shift of the warden's eyes. He excused himself to go check the records. When he was gone, Yasmin leaned down and muttered something into Rayan's ear.

"Better than ever," Rayan snapped. Yasmin frowned.

The warden was even shiftier when he returned, avoiding eye contact as he set a massive book on the table and flipped to a marked page. The script was neat, broken into sections. He pointed to a small one, only a few rows of text. "This is your witch. Angesie Bazar. Arrested June fourteenth at the Muck Moth Tavern in Jacim for the production and sale of illicit magical compounds."

"Are you wasting my time on purpose?"

The warden stilled.

"Bring us to her."

"Yes...of course, I wish I was able, Your Majesty." For such a large man, he seemed rather small. Not so frightening anymore. "The problem, well. She isn't here."

"Not here?" hissed Rayan.

"It happened six days ago. You see-"

Rayan squinted to read the tiny scrawl squeezed into the bottom of Angesie Bazar's section of the prison log.

"How," he cut the warden off, voice dipping low, "did you manage to lose a prisoner?"

"We believe an outside party aided her escape, but the method has proven itself rather blurry. There were no signs of infiltration or tampering of any sort. I assure you, these walls are protected by the strongest of charms. There is an active investigation in progress, and my officers far and wide are on the lookout for her. You have my most heartfelt apologies, Your Majesty. Trust, the situation will be resolved soon."

Rayan had stopped listening. He moved to drag his hands through his hair, then remembered himself and dropped them.

"Your arm," Yasmin said sharply, wrenching the conversation to a stop. "Show me."

Rayan cursed. "Leave," he ordered. The warden was all too happy to obey without question, taking the young man with him.

"Show me," she said again, and Nicholas realized she had been babying Rayan this entire time. Because when she gave a command - really gave one - her voice was strong enough to move a king. Rayan reluctantly stood to shed one arm of his jacket. The black shirt underneath was wet. Yasmin had spotted a tiny crimson dot on the skin between his sleeve and his glove in the second he raised his hands.

He unbuttoned the cuff, rolled up his sleeve. It clung to his skin. There was a gash in his bicep, so messy with red that Nicholas couldn't tell how deep it was.

"You need to get that treated."

"I will have it treated at home. By my doctors."

"You will have it treated here," she said in that same voice. She was at least four inches shorter and only seven years older, but there was something maternal about the way she spoke to him. Or, it was the way he visibly held back an argument, frowning like a scolded child. He nodded.

The infirmary was at the end of a dank, poorly-lit hall, near enough to the cell wing that Nicholas could hear the restlessness of the inmates. From the peek he got when the young man ushered Rayan and Yasmin in, it wasn't any more inviting on the inside. It looked more like a torture room than an infirmary. Maybe it was both.

Nicholas waited outside with the guard, who watched him intently as if he might make a run for it. From armed mages. In a prison. Nicholas refrained from any sudden movements but did lean his head against the wall, ear angled toward the door.

The walls didn't trap sound very well. If any torture did go down in that room, the sound of screaming could probably reach the inmates. Maybe that was intentional. Maybe Nicholas was thinking too much into it, like a writer.

Before any greetings could be exchanged, he heard Rayan ask, "Where are your gloves?"

"...Your Majesty?" That was a new voice. The doctor. He sounded gruff, like he could definitely torture someone.

"Your gloves. You aren't wearing gloves."

"I don't-"

Rayan's voice rose in volume. "Where are your gloves?"

"I'm...not too sure there are any, sir. But you're in good hands, swear. Please, Your Majesty, let me see your arm."

"You will not touch me."

"Your king expects that you work with gloves," Yasmin stepped in cooly. "Find some."

The door swung wide as the doctor - a beast of a man with bruised knuckles and a scarred face - scurried from the room with his tail between his legs. It closed slowly, heavy and scraping the floor. Nicholas strained his eyes to see inside.

Rayan sat at the corner of a lumpy wire bed with his eyes closed. Yasmin stood behind him. He let his head slump against her chest, and she raised her hand to cradle his face. She never normally wore gloves, but she had them on now, like she always carried a pair around with her. For his sake. Nicholas looked away before the door closed.

"When we return, tell the driver to set course for Jacim."

"I won't."

"Yaz."

"Don't," Yasmin said, firm in a way that didn't match the look he'd seen on her face. "We are going home."

"I cannot," said Rayan. "This is the only lead I have."

"And it will still be there tomorrow."

"I might not."

"Dramatic king."

"How can I be dramatic with my own life?" Nicholas couldn't hear his breath, exactly, but he could hear the way it broke up his words.

"Jacim is a rowdy city. In your state, you won't last a minute in a tavern there."

"How dare-"

Nicholas stepped away from the wall until their voices dropped away. His guard side-eyed him warily. In the end, they didn't go to Jacim.

Nicholas read alone that night. This wasn't unusual, though it had become more so over time. He had grown to expect another presence in the archive. A distracting, aggravating presence, but one that didn't say much on most nights. Nicholas had to admit - measured against the aches that came with Rayan's company, the silence wasn't so bad.

The next night found him slouched sideways on the armchair, legs dangling over the side. It wasn't comfortable. The arm dug into his spine and his neck hurt from holding the weight of his head. But he had gotten used to leaving the sofa unoccupied after dark.

It was late. Around the time that Rayan would normally leave and Nicholas would drag his heavy feet upstairs to sleep. He couldn't even remember what he was reading; the words were fogging together on the page, bleeding into large blocks of black that slowly took over his vision...

"Wake up."

Nicholas jerked awake. He tried to push himself up and wound up pushing himself right off the armchair.

"Isn't this getting a little ridiculous?" he groaned, face down on the carpet.

"I cannot hear you when you speak to the floor."

Nicholas heaved onto his back. Rayan stood above him. From this angle, he reminded Nicholas of one of those gothic clock towers, pointy and looming and feeling strangely lopsided. It was the sort of thought Nicholas would normally have in a dream. Considering he was half-asleep, he let it slide.

"It's practically morning," he said.

"I had a busy day."

So when do you sleep? Nicholas could only assume that Rayan was some sort of insomniac. That would explain the persistent shadows beneath his eyes. So really, this was all Nicholas' fault for drawing him that way. Nicholas wondered if it was related to whatever tragic past would cause a king to unravel at the simple touch of a bandit's hand. Was that also his fault, then, for always drawing Rayan with gloves?

"I've brought something."

Nicholas sat up and scooted back against the chair, wary. You could really hate me. Not just for the way he would die, but for the way he lived.

Rayan held out a porcelain figurine of a young woman sitting on a backless bench. Long hair swept down her back, merging into the black of her tunic dress. Her mouth was open, her eyes closed, like she was singing. Nicholas forgot to be skeptical or surprised. Without thinking, he reached for her.

"Don't."

He yanked his hand back.

"You'll ruin the charm," Rayan said, then muttered, "Sino dakira."

Sino. A bell charm, but not the one Malik had used to speak to Adrian from afar. Not one Nicholas knew.

A low note pulsed out from the figurine, then another. Nicholas' lips parted as the slow build took the shape of a song. Piano. Like something from a music box, except it had the muffled quality of being recorded, and it was far too complex. Too fast, too loud, the longer it went on. It kept building and building, never easing up.

It sounded...sober. Grim, but not sad. Just deep, and overcast, and frank. The musician had a straightforward style that almost felt like boasting.

"You said you weren't that good," said Nicholas.

"I said I wasn't a pianist."

"Sure sound like one."

The crinkle between Rayan's eyebrows was defensive. Nicholas recognized the music like he had recognized the king's face in that jail interrogation room so many weeks ago. The callousness of it. The understated power behind the lower notes, the restraint in the high ones. He had never heard Rayan play, but he wouldn't be convinced that this had come from anyone else. Rayan seemed to realize this. He opened his mouth to lie, then closed it again.

"You say you read faster with music," said Rayan. When Nicholas didn't comment, he kept going. "But no band. You're very demanding."

If the music's strange familiarity wasn't enough proof that the song had come straight from Rayan, the hurry to his words and the thin purse of his lips confirmed it. Flustered.

"Thank you," said Nicholas. He hauled himself onto the seat as Rayan crouched to leave the figurine on the floor. There was a moment where they were at eye level for once.

"It isn't a gift."

Rayan took a book off the new pile - they had already charged through the first - and then took the sofa. The song was lengthy; it ended with a note like a thunderclap, blunt and sudden. In the abrupt quiet afterward,

Nicholas could make out the sound of a page turning in the recording. A second song began.

The music didn't speed up his reading. Not even close. Nicholas' attention was shot.

This song was frantic. It wasn't fast, exactly, but there was urgency to it that felt...smothered. It's so him, Nicholas mused. He could almost see it. Rayan's left hand pressing slow and steady, presenting a veil of composure, while his right jumped from feverish high chords to angry lows. Deeply fucking repressed.

For all the time he spent visualizing, Nicholas' imagination could only scrounge up an incomplete image. He glanced at the sofa, at Rayan's spindly fingers splayed across the cover of his book. Look at me - it wasn't just in his eyes. Every part of him screamed it. Nicholas listened, looked, trying to picture those hands flying across the keys, corded shoulders shifting to follow them. Was he still expressionless when he played? Did he nod his head along?

The song didn't feel ominous, but it was probably supposed to. If that isn't Rayan in a nutshell.

"Focus."

Nicholas raised his eyes from Rayan's hands. I'm very focused, he thought, because he was. His face burned.

"You're frustrated."

Nicholas couldn't argue that, so he said, "Mind your business."

Rayan looked unimpressed. "Mind your manners."

"Yes, Your Majesty." Nicholas gave a sugary sweet smile.

Rayan stared, even less impressed.

"Focus," said Nicholas. Rayan's deadpan cracked. It was nearly a laugh.

The figurine cycled through a couple more songs. When the last ended, the recording restarted from the beginning, though it was tinny, less clear. This happened every time, until the music was muted and scratchy and Rayan came over for the figurine.

"You haven't eaten," he said. Nicholas' lunch and dinner trays sat on the bed upstairs, untouched.

He hadn't been able to since the attack. "I'm not hungry."

"I could hear your stomach from the sofa."

Over the music? Embarrassing.

"Worried, Your Majesty?"

Rayan took the figurine. The faded music stopped, forcing Nicholas to hear his own voice and the teasing note to it. The quiet as it hung reminded him who he was and who he was mocking. This seemed to have been Rayan's intention; he looked smug as he left. Nicholas went to sleep at dawn.